Maestro Satriano

For Tina

LeAnna DeAngelo

LeAnna DeAngelo

1. Musicians-fiction   2. Denver, Colorado-fiction
3. Satriano family-fiction   4. Italy-fiction   5. Fathers and sons-fiction
I. title

Pietro 1885

The ship is swaying, pitching, but driven by a force stronger than the current, for we are headed for America; the water from the Atlantic Ocean cannot stop the old French ship *Victoria* from her mission: to get us there.

My sister, Orsola, lies in bed a lot; she seems to be feeling poorly and does not take to the sea well. We bring her broth and try to cheer her with reminders that we will be in America soon. Since our Mother died during childbirth three years ago, Orsola has become the mama of our family. Since boarding the ship, she has said few words except, "Don't play your cornet late at night, stay out of mischief, and do not visit that sorceress lady who is on the ship. Sorcery is evil."

A sorceress lady? I cannot resist. I attend afternoon tea just long enough to hear about this sorceress and where her room is.

I immediately go to her room. She is in a small, dark room in the bowels of the ship. I am a little frightened; I have never met a sorcerer before. My brothers, Antonio and Sal, say that they can see things in the future and get their gifts from the devil. This makes visiting her all the more intriguing.

I knock on the door. Even her door seems mystical; I am unsure why. I am uncertain what to say.

She opens the door and it creaks, just like Professor Romano's door. She is dressed like a gypsy, with a long, paisley skirt and a tight-fitting blouse that shows more of her chest than Mama ever would. She answers with flair, as if she is in a musical performance. Her eyes are bright, and she projects her speech with great diction, as if performing on stage. She puts her right hand on top of the door, as if posing.

She motions for me to enter. She asks if I want a psychic reading. I nod my head yes, but am unsure what "psychic" means and what she is going to read. Because everything seems so interesting, and I am anticipating doing something so entirely taboo, I would have agreed to anything. I cannot wait to tell Sal and Antonio about my experience.

She leads me to a table that has an unusual tablecloth, with the same paisley pattern as her skirt but with some stars on it. Upon it sits a glass ball. She tells me it is a crystal ball and it tells her things others do not know. The ship is still tossing us about, and we sit but sway a bit. She holds her hands just above the ball and closes her eyes. Now, she seems to be peering into the ball, but I cannot see anything. I move closer to gaze into it with her, but she says I will not be able to see anything; only those touched by God with the gift of something called clairvoyance can. I figure she is misinformed, or has made an error, because my sister said the gift comes from the devil.

So, because I am apparently not given a gift from either hell or heaven, I try to sit back and relax. She closes her eyes tightly again, as if what she is seeing is too much for her. A long time goes by, it seems. She begins speaking in a different voice. It seems so scary I almost run out of the room.

"You are starting on a great journey into an unknown territory. There was a death in your family...your Mother, I think? You have been very sad. You will be well known and many people will talk about you years after your death. You will bring happiness to many people. You have great talent, God-given talent, and you will share it with others throughout your long life. You have a temper and will have problems in relationships. Tread lightly, my dear boy, and you will be loved for your talent. You are not a peasant or a farmer, I can tell that by your hands. You come from an elitist family…"

She closes her eyes again, and then gets up from the table carefully because the ship is still tossing us to and fro. She scrunches her eyes together and shakes her head, as if trying to let go of her visions, and then proclaims, as if an actress on stage making her final statement, "And that is what I see at this time." Then she opens her eyes suddenly, as if she has just awakened from a dream, and ushers me toward the door. She again puts one hand on her hip and the other on the top of the doorframe, as if posing. "Good-bye, young man. I will not charge you."

And with that she closes her mystical door, and I do not see her again for the rest of the voyage.

Part One
1882–1889

CHAPTER ONE

"He was known as one in the front rank of Italian
composers of classical music, and as probably the man
best versed in the art of arranging classical music in
his country..."

Antonio 1882

I sit at my desk at the University of Italy in Naples, the loss of
my wife still gripping me through my heart and my spine. I
look at my hands, aware that my throat is tight, my eyes sensitive
and moist. I loved her more than I had known...how can I
forgive myself, a romantic composer? Should I not suffer more?
It is the man who inseminates the woman and causes the baby to
grow in her womb. Looking at my hands, I cannot help but think
I caused her to die. How could the beauty of new life be swept
away by the swiftness of death? She knew she was dying; she told
me so. I lied to her and said she would be fine; the lie haunts me
more than anything. She died knowing I was dishonest with her.
I glance at my cornet, my only solace since Letizia's death. The
cornet comes alive at the time of death.

I look at my hands again, looking older. I notice people look
at their hands when they are devastated, when they seek solace.
Letizia will never know old age. What would she have wanted for
me, for the children?

I look at my black suit and trousers. Branches and twigs brush against the window. My sisters do the laundry and cooking for my family now, an extra burden for them. So many worries. I get up from my desk and walk into the hall, my favorite place to be. The cellos reverberating, the syncopation alternating asynchronously. The pianos tinkling, and the trumpets, an instrument that seems to call out from an unknown place. If God could create these sounds, why did he take Letizia, and why can he not soothe me? The Music Department has been my sanctuary; it holds the power of music. If it were not for music and my children, I may be tempted not to go on. Letizia walks with me through the halls. Centuries of the most beautiful music, the most sacred songs ever created, have wafted through these halls.

I quickly must regain my composure, because here comes my friend, Professor Andotti, walking toward me.

"Antonio, the death of your wife saddens me. It must be very hard on you and your children. May God be with you."

We turn toward a window, a small amount of light shining through clouds.

"I appreciate your condolences, but they are useless, my friend; nothing can reach my grief."

"You will navigate your way. Your heart, your music, and Letizia's music will show you the way, guided by God."

Was it my imagination or did the sky brighten a bit? Somehow, with the combination of my friend's caring and the sun shining for a rare moment, I feel slightly better. The thought of navigating a new path with Letizia's spirit and music is inspiring.

After her death, we moved into my sister's house, where we now sit at my brother-in-law's table for meals. My brother-in-law is a kind man, but I feel awkward about intruding. I feel uncomfortable in his home, and restless from my despair.

To assuage my grief, I walk along the shore, the clouds of Naples serving as bleak solace again. The clouds are familiar and provide a type of celestial ritual, yet the sun also provides comfort in a different way. I hear that it is sunnier in America. In the distance, I see a ship, perhaps bound there. I remind myself that although grieving, I am still a free man. I used to dream of going to America, a new land with the promise of freedom. Some of my colleagues have already left, hoping to find fame in the Land of the Free. I frequently receive letters from colleges and universities in America. They need musicians; the Jesuit schools especially desire Italian musicians so that America can have an excellent tradition of music and can propagate America with plenty of Jesuits.

At Letizia's funeral one of my elderly aunts said to me, quite flustered "Antonio, your poor children, they lived without you while you were serving General Garibaldi in the war , and now your children are without their Mama, too." She looked down, closed her eyes and shook her head back and forth, then raised her hands and gesticulated dramatically "Ah…and Pietro, living away from home for so long, and now living without a mama." It is true, although it makes me angry. My children deserve the best, and staying in Italy may not be what is best for them.

The sea air feels strong, punitive and nurturing all at the same time. Professor Andotti's words float through my mind. *You will find your way, your music, and Letizia's spirit will guide you*, are my thoughts as I walk the shore, and before returning to my sister's house, I take one last glimpse at the sea that guides the ship carrying lost souls to America. The ship, heading west, seems to call to me.

When I was eight, my mother always told me my imagination would lead me to either be a fool or a musician. I countered that music would lead my imagination. Such lonely thoughts now, as Mama, Papa and Letizia have now passed.

I remember well when I served as a sergeant for General Giuseppe Garibaldi, the liberator of Italy. My love of adventure, of the unknown, led me afar, to unknown places. Oh, how I miss the excitement of battle, traveling and working hard and witnessing life and death. After a while, they seemed one, life and death, a narrow continuum. I very much admired General Garibaldi, who was willing to sacrifice the lives of some, with certainty that it would lead to a better world.

As a young soldier, I fought battles and traveled with Garibaldi, a courageous and progressive leader. If he had been an entertainer, his magnetism and presence would have made him great, for just his presence acquiesced foes and charmed servants, but there was another man in him, too. He hired me as a sergeant, but I would perform for him, too. He loved Verdi and Rossini. He could become quite emotional during performances; his eyes glazing over, he would weep or sometimes laugh and dance. For all his bravado, he had a sentimental side.

There is an oft-told story about Garibaldi and his men encountering a sheepherder who lost a lamb. There is a similar story that I played a role in. Late one night, while returning to our base, it was raining and very cold. A man said he could not find his wife and baby. They went to visit relatives and had not returned. Garibaldi commanded us to search for them, and we all went in different directions. After a few hours, we regrouped in the freezing rain, but Garibaldi was nowhere to be found and we returned without him or the lady and baby. I was quite concerned about all of them, but we figured he was still searching, and he would search until he found them. In the morning, I checked to see if he had returned. Normally one to rise with the sun and roosters, there he was, sleeping soundly in his bed. My movements awakened him. He smiled coyly, and got up from bed, and opened the door to an adjacent room. The lady and baby were in bed, sound asleep. He got back into his own bed, and I took this to mean I should take leave and allow them all to rest quietly.

I do not return to my office, but instead go back to my room at my sister's home. My son, Pietro, enters the room. Does my son really know who I am? He sees me as his Papa. But I am also a grieving husband, a music professor, a genteel artist, and part of the intellectual class of Italy.

Why these stories seem important to share with Pietro, my musical heir, with whom I am close, I am unsure. I believe Pietro has the most talent of all my sons. I guess every man wants his life experiences to be known to his children; it is the only immortality that really exists. Playing cornet, writing waltzes and operas, and rearranging some of Verdi's work was grand. I have accomplished much in the years I have been given, but always I want more. I suppose every man fantasizes about immortality.

Pietro returned home from the Royal Academy of Music in Milan when his mother died. When he was eight, he cried for days upon being told his rare talent put him in the classification of a child prodigy, a genius, and he would leave for the Academy, traveling by stagecoach, within a few weeks.

Letizia was saddened by the separation, too, but I assured her that he needed to study with the best. Our son could be famous. Letizia disagreed and thought the boy should live at home until he was older, but I would hear nothing of it.

Watching Pietro walk through the door, I regret my assertion that he should live in Milan. Women know best about children; why did I not listen to Letizia? I remind myself that this is yet another time when he needs softness now, not hardness.

Pietro has talent; it pours forth when he plays. He has the presence of a leader like Garibaldi, but the boyish magnetism of a young, gifted performer. People tell me I, too, had the same characteristics. Pietro is disciplined for a young man, unusually so, as if the cornet were all that existed. The Greeks said there were two types of charisma: personality charisma and divinely conferred charisma. Colleagues and I believe he has both.

I have resumed practicing with him every evening at seven thirty, the time we practiced together before he went to Milan. I feel guilty making the boy practice when he is grieving so, but he seems eager to play. Yesterday, just minutes into his lesson, I told him we did not have to practice; we were both too upset and should pray and retire early. He looked sullen, his lower lip extending as if to cry. I had expected him to be relieved, but instead we sat there in silence, both of us staring at our cornets.

Then I realized he wanted to play, needed to play. We played softly at first. A tearful, slow melody with more emotion than I have ever heard in all my days. The music was all we had. We played for hours, without speaking in words. We played softly and slowly, long into the night.

Now that he has been home for a week, the boy's fervor has diminished, although slightly, and I knew his heart was healing from his Mother's death. I told Pietro, somewhat reluctantly, that he should go back to Milan soon, to resume his studies. "Si, Papa" was his only response.

The next day, I awake feeling more energized than I have since Letizia's death. I say good morning to my daughters and my sister. Even when I see my brother-in-law at his table, I do not feel as awkward, and our living situation feels more natural.

At the university, I go to the tallest tower at the university. I think of Copernicus, in Milan centuries ago, exploring the sea and devising a theory that the earth was round, not flat. Simultaneously with this thought, the notion enters my mind that because of Copernicus, my family could move to the New World, across the ocean. I look out over the university, one of the oldest and most revered in the world. I look out to sea, to the west, and though there is no ship to engage my vision, I have a thought that buoys me: my children and I will move to America. Pietro will need to stay in Milan for now, to gain even more mastery and eminence. Then, they will join me and have a wonderful life as musicians, and will not be stuck behind these decaying walls with no freedom. Garibaldi told me stories about living in America in the 1850s. He loved it there. I strive to emulate his sense of adventure, his sense of grandness, both for himself and the world. It must have been contagious, like the invisible spirits said to make one ill, for I caught from him a love of adventure.

I enjoy being among the most highly regarded composers and music professors in all of Italy; I love the musical nights when the opera houses keep their gas lamps lit late into the night, and the celebrations with kings and queens and the pageantry of the performances. I love all of this, but felt restless even before Letizia died; it started when I was teaching. The music that is pervasive in my daily life is grand and takes me to far places even on the darkest days, but I miss the *sturm und drang*.

Those letters I receive every month from America wanting musicians keep weighing on my mind. The government wants us to leave, in fact needs people to leave, especially southern Neapolitans, whose cholera outbreaks have been severe. The government does not have enough money to support everyone, and more money is going to northern Italy rather than to southern Italy. It is difficult to grow crops after centuries of farming, and the outlook here in southern Italy is very bleak.

Since unification, the government has been encouraging immigration of its people to alleviate these economic pressures. The College of the Sacred Heart in a place called Denver, and the University of San Francisco, both have asked me to move to the New World and be a music professor.

I am a religious man but see God in music, and music only.

Pietro

I go to the bedroom my brothers and I share. My brothers are not home, probably out swimming or doing their studies. The room is in the attic, with large plank wood on the floors and wooden rafters and whitish stucco walls. The acoustics in the room are good for music. I flop down on the bed my brothers Antonio, Salvatore and I share. Lying on my stomach, I feel lonely for them, and the current aloneness will be a permanent one as soon as I leave again for Milan. This room is comforting to me. My brothers would play, argue, have pillow fights, giggle and whisper. The room seems so silent now. And where am I going? Back to Milan, where I will practice hours a day and mentor students, sitting with perfect posture in a hard wooden chair, or standing for hours conducting and performing.

Silence in this house was an infrequent visitor when Mama was alive and I lived here with my brothers and sisters. Orsola and Concetta both play the piano, plus all the other music Papa and my brothers created.

I had to leave my family and friends because I am so talented. I used to think *how could music cause this to happen*? I felt as if music had betrayed me. Maybe I do not like music after all, I thought; it has double-crossed me, or maybe my parents were the ones who double-crossed me by leading me to think music is the epitome of life, the ultimate and only goal in life. If my musical talent caused me to be so different from everyone else, perhaps it is an unwise and disadvantageous pursuit.

I will forever be haunted by the memory of my Mother's casket being lowered into the ground. The last few years, I was unable to spend time with her because I was away at school; music severed a bond.

Another haunting memory comes to me: After I had been a student in Milan for several years, the Spanish royal family requested that I be a musician to King Alphonso XII of Spain. The King was young, just slightly older than me, and very ill with consumption. They wanted the young King to have a companion as well as a musician. Papa said it was a great honor and a rare opportunity, and I should leave at once and say *arrivederci* to my friends and professors before I left. By this time, I had finally adjusted to being at the Royal Academy of Music and loved it there and wanted to stay, but also felt like I did not have a choice.

I was sad about moving again, and believed I was at the Royal Academy of Music for the last time. The person I was closest to was Professor Romano.

Old Professor Romano was withered, bent over and shaky. Many of the other students were afraid of him, but he had a sparkle in his eye and treated me like someone special. One time he told me I have so much talent, God blessed me many times over. Professor Romano never struck my hands when I played a mischievous note, like other professors do. I remember going to say goodbye to him, thinking I would probably not see him again.

I opened Professor Romano's door, and it creaked in the pitch of G. He was sitting in his rocking chair, with the music stand in front of him and his cornet close by, at the ready. He motioned for me to come to his side. The first night here, when I was only eight, I missed Mama and Papa so, and Professor Romano held me tenderly, like a papa. That day, I kneeled before him and he placed his hands on my head, "Pietro, never forget you are gifted, and you must share your gift. Never let anyone tell you otherwise." Then, he put his hands on my face. His hands smelled of flowers and vino. He kissed my cheeks and sat back. I then understood that I was to kiss him, too. His whiskers felt bristly like straw, yet soft like his cheeks. He was teary eyed, and it seemed scary. I had never seen Papa cry. I did not want to go to Spain, and wanted to stay with Professor Romano forever. He took a ring off his finger and put it in my hands by clasping my right hand first, then my left hand, and then gently opening my fingers. It was gold with diamonds, and I remember it seemed soft at the time.

"You go now, my child, and I will visit you someday in America." I wondered why he thought I would live in America. I stare at the ring. "It was given to me by my favorite professor. It has magical qualities and will keep you safe on your voyage, and beyond."

I would have to live with this gift, and this parting, for the rest of my life, I remember thinking at that moment.

I ran out the door, feeling *pazzo*, crying, like a madman stuck in a dream. I looked at the ring, and it made me feel even more like a lunatic. I ran through the kitchen and saw a bottle. I grabbed it. It is mine. I stole it. It felt good. I ran faster, sweating. The chef ran out into the hall. "Boy, bring back my goose fat! I cannot cook the evening meal without it!" I laughed like a fool and loved it.

I wanted that goose fat more than I ever wanted anything. I had no idea what it was or what to do with it. But something big was being taken from me, so I took something small. It felt like mine, and I liked it more than the ring.

I served as a musician to King Alphonso for about two years. He was tired frequently. It was sad, because he was so young and we were friends, and I liked knowing I brought happiness to his short life. He died at age 27, shortly after I arrived in America.

After he died, because I had been a good student, and then became a musician to royalty, I was asked to return to Milan as a salaried instructor at the Royal Academy of Music. I suspect Professor Romano was influential in this decision. I left Spain to return there, where I became a peer to my professors, although part of me still felt like a student and a schoolboy in their presence. Professor Romano assured me it was common to feel that way, and it may not ever go away.

My thoughts return to the present, to this room. Last night, Papa told me he is planning to move to America. After three years of employment, he can send for me and my brothers and sisters to move there as well. I will think about it. There are so many opportunities in America, yet I have so many opportunities here already. If I am to pursue the path of a brilliant musician and professor, why risk it all; why not stay here?

Antonio

I have written letters to all the performance theatres in New York and have secured a job as a composer. I will depart in a few months, earn some money in New York, and then continue west. I shall be a vagabond musician. I feel bad about leaving my family, especially my son Salvatore, who lost his mother at age ten. Now, he will be without his Papa, too, but Orsola and Concetta are young women now; in addition to all the aunts and Letizia's parents, he will be fine. He needs to study music more like Pietro and my other son, Antonio, and I should like for him to study at a conservatory as well, just like Pietro.

For some reason, at the moment I think this last thought, my mind is fixed: I shall accept the professorship in San Francisco. My decision helps me feel better. I feel as though my fate has changed course; I have cast my ambitions upward and onward and am leaving myself free to the wind of the open sea, which will blow me west to America, and perhaps back again, as I will eventually return to accompany my children on their voyage to the New World.

CHAPTER TWO

"…When he landed in New York,
he was recognized as a genuine artist…"

5 March 1882
Francesco Basile
Italian Consul
Kansas City, Missouri

Dear Signor Basile,

I hope you and your family are well. My wife died two months ago, during childbirth. I know that you are highly respected now as an Italian immigration adviser in Kansas City, Missouri. I seek passage to the United States of America. Please make clearance for me to leave in the spring, on the earliest ship possible for safe passage after the winter storms. I would like to settle in New York, the closest point to Europe, and will work for three years, then send for my children. Ultimately, I would like to go to California. The University of San Francisco has sent me letters inquiring whether I am interested in teaching at a Jesuit college, and that is agreeable in the future, but I do not want to travel that far without my children at this time.

Yours sincerely,

Professor A. Satriano, University of Italy

31 March, 1882
Prof. A. Satriano
University of Italy, Naples

Dear Professor Satriano,

I am sorry to hear your wife has gone to heaven. The United States is divine; there is open land, although also prejudice, especially in large cities, against Italians. When you are ready to travel farther west, I can secure passage for you through to Kansas City, Missouri, and likely all the way to Denver, Colorado, if you desire. Denver is a beautiful, healthy, very small settlement with surrounding mountains. The town is growing, and I hear that officials want to increase its cultural venues for society, and to make it a modern city, equivalent to the well-established large cities in the eastern part of America; they are attempting to accentuate the area's healthy environment with corresponding culture and wealth. The river that runs through Denver is the Platte River so it is known as Paris on the Platte.

Travel across America is long and slow. The trains go all the way to California, but Kansas City and Denver will be good resting spots before meeting the ocean at the edge of the world in California.

You will set sail on the *Victoria* on 29 April 1882. Godspeed.

Yours most kindly,

Francesco Basile

Italian Immigrant Adviser

Kansas City, Missouri, United States of America

Pietro 1884

I have been a professor at the Academy and the leader of a marching band for a year now, and it has now been almost two years since Papa left for America.

Late one night, I walk into an old concert hall at the conservatory. I need to compose and love the organ in this particular building, built in the 1500s. The building smells sweet and musty, of old wood.

Few people venture into this decadent building, but on this night I hear a young soprano voice singing softly in the dark, with just one candle lit on stage. She suddenly stops singing, apparently when she hears the door close behind me. She runs.

I call out to her, but she does not answer.

I light some of the lamps, to see if I can illuminate the voice I heard.

I look between the wooden rafters and walk around, trying to find this young lady. Through the darkness, I see large brown eyes across the hall. She is a very short girl with massive hair. She sees me and runs again. She cannot open the old door quickly enough. I run to her.

"What is your name?"

"Anna, sir." She is trembling.

I wonder who she is and where she came from.

"Are you a student here?"

"No." And she walks out into the dark night and seems to disappear into the mist.

I keep up my work, composing and teaching, but my mind always drifts to Anna. Her tiny figure that of a doll, or a ballerina, and that hair flowing, flowing and encompassing her. She looks exotic. She comes here, hiding among the rafters, singing, possibly hoping to be discovered, but shy, and here I am, the man who can help her. I will make sure Anna gets to sing in the Great Hall. I am excited, so excited, nothing else seems important.

Months and months go by. The moon grows and then wanes. The students file through, spending their days singing or performing and then move on to work or to study at other conservatories. I keep going to the auditorium at strange times, trying to find her there. Was she my imagination, a phantom diva in the old opera house?

Then, one night at about midnight, as I am walking up the stairs to enter the grand room, I hear a girl's high, sweet soprano voice. Hauntingly passionate. Her voice reminds me of innocence with a touch of flame. She gazes at me with her vulnerable eyes and stops singing.

"Signora Anna! It is so good to see you." I speak very softly because I am afraid that if I speak too loud, she will vanish into the mist again.

"Signor Satriano." She curtsies.

"Please, please, continue to sing. Then perhaps we can walk around the campus. It is a lovely evening." She looks down and smiles coyly. Her timidity increases my timidity.

I was a musician to King Alphonso of Spain and was taught by the old masters. Now I am the leader of a military marching band, and I am hardened. I can be brash; that is what musical training is like in Italy. But Anna makes me feel like I have to control myself, not everyone else, and it is refreshing to be with her. She makes me feel like Pietro, not Maestro Satriano.

She sings "Ave Maria" and "Mio Bambino Caro" and her timbre and pitch are *benissimo*. I am mesmerized by her beauty. And, also afraid someone will find us. How would I explain being alone with this wisp of a girl at one in the morning? Every little creak of the old wood and mud building makes me think the night guard is coming.

After she sings, we walk and walk, among the vineyards beneath a full moon. She allows me to take her hand.

"How old are you, Anna?"

"Too young to be with you, Maestro." She says it in her innocent, yet flirtatious, kind of way.

"Well, how young is too young?"

"I am but a child, and you are attracted to me." She smiles.

"Si, I am."

"I am fourteen, Maestro." And with that, she stops talking, grabs my lapel, and draws me near. "I am not a nice girl."

"Oh, quite the contrary, I think you are."

"Then you must be a bad boy. How old are you?"

"Twenty." I refrain from addressing her other comment.

We kiss in the moonlight and hold hands until dawn; it was all pretty innocent.

The next day I tell the headmaster I found a girl with a beautiful voice, and I would like for her to perform. He says, "Ah, Professor Satriano, what is her name?"

"Anna."

"Well, what is her last name?"

"I do not know, sir."

"She is a student here and you do not know her name?"

"No. She...lives nearby and I heard her singing..."

"We cannot let a person sing who is not officially enrolled here."

"But sir, you must hear her. May I schedule a time for her to give an audition?"

"Who is her father, and how did you meet this girl?"

"Sir, let us not get entangled with details..."

He seems irritated. "How old is she?"

"Well, sir...she is probably quite young."

I am feeling foolish. Here I am, a professor at the Royal Academy of Music, and I am trying to court a very young lady I am smitten with.

Professor Amira takes a few puffs of his cigar. He looks out over the old auditorium, inhales deeply. He seems to be imagining an audience, as if we are on stage. I can tell these are his imaginings, for suddenly he sits up straighter and speaks louder with more elocution:

"Maestro Satriano, with all due respect...this could get you into trouble. She is but a mere child. You could have any lady you wanted in Italy. I have never heard of this girl...keep your wits about you."

"And with all due respect to you, Professor Amira, matters of my personal life are my own..."

"Just like your father. You speak your mind."

Taking my cue from him, imagining what an audience would think about this conversation, I stand, facing away from him and toward the seats of the grand music hall where Verdi and Vivaldi performed, and the acoustics are grand. "My professional opinion is that she has great musical talent. All I ask is a guest appearance at the next recital. She will sing "The Holy City." I guarantee you that everyone will be impressed."

Professor Amira walks toward me at the edge of the stage. We turn toward each other, as if a great theatrical dialogue were about to unfold. He looks me in the eye. He has those wayward eyebrows that men get when they are older. They seem to have a life all their own, in some ways more expressive and distracting than the eyes. His eyebrows are so unusual, I find myself looking at them instead of into his eyes. "My boy, just be careful. The young ladies can cause catastrophes in a man's life." And then he walks away.

The date is set for her to perform at the next student recital a few weeks later on March 10. Because I only know her first name, and she is quite mysterious, I do not know where she lives. I cannot call on her or ask her parents' permission. She seems like someone who does not have parents, although maybe she does. I go to the old recital hall, day and night, trying to catch her to give her the news that she will be able to perform with an orchestra. I wander there on sleepless nights in my nightclothes carrying a lantern, or go there with my lunch between rehearsals with the marching band. I start to lose hope, when suddenly, sitting at my desk one day eating spaghetti, there she is.

When I tell her the news, she is genuinely excited. She gives me a brief kiss on the cheek, which makes me excited in a different kind of way. She is talking about a beautiful dress she will wear, and twirls about as if she is a ballerina when describing its different features, and how she will wear her hair. Her quixotic hair will look beautiful any way she decides to wear it.

March 10 comes and goes, and she does not show up. Who is this girl who captured my imagination so? The orchestra and Professor Amira waited for this girl, written in the playbill as only "Anna," but she never came. Is she a phantom; could she exist only in my imagination? Again, I wonder, could she be unreal, just a fantasy nymph with a beautiful voice?

Professor Amira is quite upset with me. A few days later, I receive a letter from Papa and he asks whether I want to live in America, and I agree. A new start without tantalizing, imaginary miniature singers sounds good. I wonder whether my contract here as professor would be renewed anyway, due to, as the French would say, my faux pas.

Little did I know, even after setting sail to America, this was by no means my last encounter with Anna. She would come back to haunt me again.

CHAPTER THREE

*"He began music lessons at the age of 6,
and continued studying under the best
band masters until he reached manhood."*

Antonio

I boarded the ship on the 22 of April, 1882. My children, cousins, colleagues from the university and members of my late wife's family gather to bid me farewell. It is a bittersweet time of memories and whispered fond adieus, one of those moments one never forgets in life. So many of them wished they could come with me, but their deep roots in the Mother Land, their families, and their fears prevent them from starting anew. Adventure, somehow, is in my blood, and my quest to help Pietro, Salvatore, and Antonio have the best life possible as musicians in a free world stoke my determination. And, I, too, want to expand my musical experiences.

After a while, the formality of *arrivederci* and prayers serve only to make me want to leave and get away from this old land.

Shortly after my arrival in New York, I am saddened by the news that General Garibaldi died. People in New York hold vigils in his honor, and it is all the talk in New York, but I have not met anyone else here who served under him. I take a ferry to Staten Island, where he lived in exile for a period of time, and worked as a candle maker.

I court some fine ladies, and several more are interested, but I remain true to Letizia, my children, and being a musician.

My life in New York is splendid, but I am only able to get contract work. I dine with the best and work at an opera house on a street called Broadway, and elsewhere. Life is at a faster pace here than in Italy; although I enjoy the briskness and aliveness, I find myself drinking more gin than ever. I compose, perform, eat, drink gin and sleep. I work intensely and write some good pieces. Some of my compositions are for hire, so I do not get credit for them, but am paid a handsome sum.

Part of me would love to stay in New York; in fact, it may be best for my career to stay. There is a sense here that New York has attained the epitome of modern society, and opportunities are always expanding and emerging.

New York is very similar, in my opinion, to London. People came to build a new world, but what they have created is not too different from the old one. I still have the wanderlust and want to go to the part of America that is still forming, still fresh and new, and bring opera and other Italian music to the rural people in what is known as the Wild West.

CHAPTER FOUR

"...A cornet virtuoso..."

Antonio 1885

I return to Naples and to gather my family and we leave Italy in late May of 1885 on an old French ship. I am not as worried about my voyage across the Atlantic as I was the first time; this time my children shall be with me and I can help them adjust to sea life and life in America; it would have been harder on me and on them if they had come with me the first time.

Our parting is much the same as the first time I left, with my family and Letizia's gathered at the port, bidding us a safe voyage. An old priest says prayers. We are given plenty of food for the voyage, although there is plenty of food on the ship. Coming back to Italy enabled me to get more music and other things I needed. In my haste the first time, I did not bring my baton, which belonged to my grandfather, who was a highly esteemed musician also. When I returned to Italy, I searched at the University, but no one had seen it. I do truly miss my baton; I was going to pass it on to Pietro.

My daughters, Orsola and Concetta, are a bit timid and a bit more fearful about the voyage and leaving Italy. Perhaps they have less to gain in America; perhaps their feminine dispositions make them want to be with family, and I feel some remorse about taking them away. They have each other, and some rambunctious brothers to help create some folly and purpose in their lives, for now. I will have Francesco Basile send a wife to me from Italy as soon as we are established, both for my needs and for the needs of my daughters.

The seas quickly turn rough once we leave the Italian coast. Soon we are all sick and vomiting, my younger children retching and crying.

"We are on an adventure!" I keep reminding them, but their looks make me feel poorly about my enthusiasm. I believe the boys and I should continue our lessons on the ship, to maintain some sense of normalcy. We will practice together at 7:30 pm before the evening meal, if we are able to partake of it.

We are in steerage, my musician's salary not allowing for anything more. There are rats, and bugs that hiss, fly, crawl, and vex us. There is vomit, the smell of rot and unclean bodies everywhere. There seems to be a very slow leak through a very minute hole on the left side of the ship, and at times I secretly wonder whether it is a selfish, foolish idea to put my family in such danger.

Throughout the journey, my children develop fevers and rashes, they cry in the night, and there is no mama to hold them tight. I curse myself for following my dreams for a better life. As the ship rocks to and fro, and at times sounds like it is being ripped apart, my nightmares are of my children dying. What if one of them dies from this torrential sea? Would I not suffer in hell for eternity or beyond? What was I thinking? Mama told me my imagination would either lead me to be a musician or a fool, and at this black, dark hour, watching my children wretch, cry, delirious with pain, I know I am a fool. A fool of a man to put my children in such danger just to because I have wanderlust. Why leave my stable, prestigious job to go to the unknown? All men in all times likely question their dreams: Galileo, King Solomon, Napoleon, Columbus and Darwin risked all, and I am sure they believed their risks paid off. What would Letizia think right now? Would she be cursing me and my ancestors, crying and delirious with fever, just like the children?

Her constitution was always fragile. If she were still alive, I could not do this. Maybe she is watching over us, and she will protect us and bless our voyage. I can only hope and pray this is true.

The storm eventually passes, and so does the sickness of my children. They are now fine, and are starting to be restless on the ship. They run the decks, steal oranges from the kitchen, and my oldest boy, Pietro, is flirting with the young ladies, boasting about himself and his accomplishments as a swimmer, fisherman, cornet and trumpet player.

Pietro is always a bit pensive, a bit abrupt in his dealings with people. He enjoys teaching the younger children on the ship about music, he is pedantic, and less of a free spirit than his brothers. One thing I cannot understand is that he has a jar of something that appears to be cooking grease, and he will not let go of it. I have reassured him that there is plenty of fat on the ship to cook, and there will be fat in America, but he leaves the jar next to him on the nightstand at night and puts it in his coat pocket during the day. He seems to need it, and I suppose I should not try to wrestle it out of his hands. My other children tease him about it. I think of them as my children, but Orsola is now twenty-three and Salvatore, my youngest, is fourteen.

There are people on the ship who are returning to America. One gentleman, a Giuseppe Fiornio, was in America for a few years, but returned to Italy because his wife was so unhappy and missed her family. He seems as if he is from a foreign land, his brief time in America having transformed him; I wonder, have I changed from my brief time in America? After a few years in Italy, his wife died and he is now free to return to America. He speaks English very well, and I have invited him to dine with the captain and me tonight. The irony of being a musician is that you travel in steerage but the captain wants to dine with you, and you are the only person in steerage the captain pays attention to. But I digress; I would like for the children to spend time with Giuseppe; otherwise, we will not be able to accomplish much in the New World.

Salvatore plays the tuba; he is a night owl and practices when the lanterns are burning. I tell him not to, that he is disturbing people, but he continues, an example of the stubbornness that seems pervasive in the Satriano family. Or, maybe it is the elusive muse of music that allures us to be immersed and lost in music, no matter the consequences.

My daughters knit and talk to Signora Pictorelli, who is also planning to travel from New York to Kansas City. I am glad my daughters have found her; she is a kind and gentlewoman, and good with my younger children, and is just the person they need. She is like a mama to them, and reminds them to be good young ladies. She tells them stories and tends to their feminine needs.

The captain of the ship has asked us to perform in a fortnight, and we will do so with pleasure. The sea will be calm that night, he assures me. The passengers could use some morale building, as two people in steerage have died from fever or starvation. "And by the time we reach America," he says, "more souls will have lost their lives to the ravages of the sea."

Again, I thank God for keeping my family safe from harm. In my mind, I quickly recite, *In the name of the Father, the Son, and the Holy Ghost, Amen.*

Then I remember something I want to ask the captain.

"Sir, at times I see a ship on the horizon, behind us."

"Si, Professor Satriano. That is the French ship *Isere*. It is hauling what is known as the Statue of Liberty in 214 wooden crates. It will probably reach New York Harbor a day after us."

CHAPTER FIVE

"Professor Satriano, a distinguished leader
and composer of music."

Pietro

We arrive in New York just before dawn on June 16, 1885. Papa awakens us and says, "We have reached America!" I thought he was joking; it did not seem possible after all this time that we finally arrived. It is dark and foggy, but I can see some land. We all walk to the port side of the ship in our nightclothes and see where the Statue of Liberty is going to be placed. I imagine what it will soon be like for immigrants: a lady, supposedly holding a torch, to welcome and light the way. In Europe, I never saw a statue on the water, so I already know America is an unusual place.

Now, in the wee hours of the morning, my brothers and I talk about living in America. We are hopeful but wary. Regardless, we must be brave. There is no turning back, really.

Antonio

We arrive at Castle Garden in New York. The boys and I are able to speak English to the immigration officer. He is impressed, and admires my suit and our instruments. He asks both my daughters questions in English, and they do not respond. He looks at me and winks, knowing it is unimportant for young women to speak

English. The children are happy to be off the ship. We will stay in New York for a month. People say New York is the most similar to Europe than any other part of America because it is the largest city, except that the musical community is close and tight-knit, and it feels like a small country rather than a conglomeration of some of the most talented people in the world.

CHAPTER SIX

"I can remember my mother (Orsola) telling me
it took them twenty days to cross the ocean
in a wooden French ship."
Author's family documents, from Josephine Cona (D'Angelo)

Pietro

On June 17, we stand with thousands of people and watch the *Isere* arrive in New York Harbor. Ironically, the Statue of Liberty is supposed to greet immigrants, but instead, we greet her.

On the streets of New York, there are crowds everywhere and people yelling in languages I have never heard. Everyone seems to be in a hurry and many people seem to be angry, for some reason. One man calls us niggers. I am unsure what that means, but by the look on his face, it is a bad thing. Another man says, "People from Africa cannot be here! You in wrong part of the city." Another woman, dressed like a gypsy, stands very close to Papa and puts her arms around him and asks him if he wants her to dance for him in private. I do not understand this.

More than anything, everyone here seems busy, and there are lots of rules and many different and unusual aromas of food wafting through the air. All people seem to be working; the streets are orderly and straight, and everyone seems quite serious compared to home. What is similar to Italy is the sea, and the ships that come here every day. Papa says we will not be in New York for long, and that we should eat a lot of fish from the sea, because the sea will be far from where we are going.

There are people with lots of different hair colors, and people who are taller than people are in Italy. We are staying in the Italian part of the city. Mrs. Pictorelli will stay with us a few days. She reminds me of Mama. At night, people light a fire in the street with wood and people play all kinds of instruments—guitars, saxophones, accordions, harmonicas, and of course my brothers on clarinet and tuba, and Papa and I with our cornets. Many of the houses and buildings here are made of wood. There are grand buildings like at home, too. I still wish I were in Milan; I am uncertain of this new life.

Papa keeps telling me to get rid of this jar of goose fat, but I just cannot let go of it.

After a month in New York, we board a train for Kansas City from Grand Central Station. My brothers and sisters are excited, and we get on the train quickly and find seats in the first car. A man comes around collecting tickets and says, "Please go to the Negro Car."

"We are not Negroes, we are Italians, sir," Papa speaks up. "I believe we have the right to sit here; we are musicians, and these are my children—Orsola, Concetta, Pietro, Antonio, and Salvatore." I should not call them my children; most of them are young adults now, but to me they are always my children.

The conductor seems to be having second thoughts about the need to move us to the back of the train, but then says, "Italians are not much better than Negroes. Please go to the back of the train."

I thought Papa wanted to come here because we would be treated better and have more opportunities. Papa thinks the conductor is a good man just doing his job, and he may have been concerned we have diseases that other people in the United States may not have.

I spend most of the trip looking out the window at the vast land, with hills and hills, and then more hills and more hills, with an occasional farm in the distance. I wonder what it is like to live so far away from everyone and everything.

When people see our instruments they ask us to play songs. It is a Sunday, and we play some hymns, just so people on the train will not think we are complete heathens. Even that surly conductor smiles and lingers in the Negro section when we play "Nearer My God to Thee."

20 July 1885

Dear Professor Romano,

Thank you for your letter. It only took three weeks to arrive, and Papa could not believe we got here so quickly.

I played first trumpet with the Cincinnati Symphony. The musicians were all encouraging. They said, "Boy, you are going to be famous." Papa worked for the symphony briefly, but we are moving on now to a place called Kansas City, where Papa will again work for an operatic company. America is different from what I thought it would be. There are fewer people here and no castles, and all the buildings are new. Most of America looks like the countryside of Italy. The food is very different; some of it is good and some of it I have no desire for.

I practice daily and remember all that you taught me.

Your humble student,

P. Satriano

15 December 1885

My Dear Pietro Antonio,

Your letter arrived in good shape, *grazie* for sharing so much of your adventure in America. You mentioned different foods and people from all over the world. I do wonder, is the music different as well? I would love to hear about the music played there. With the many different religions and cultures, the music in churches and synagogues would be intriguing; try to listen to many different types of music.

It is interesting that you brought the goose fat with you. I am sure you are up to great mischief in America.

I will plan to visit you in America, when you are a famous cornetist in the New World.

Yours,

Professor G. Romano

Royal Academy of Music, Milan

I wonder whether Professor Romano really will come to America? He seems too old, seemed like someone who has never left Milan and never should. He belongs there, of the Old World, not here.

I fall asleep, holding the letter in my hand.

We arrived in Kansas City, Missouri, today.

As soon as we alight the train, it is obvious that Kansas City is different from New York and Italy. *It feels different.* The aroma of dampness and fertile soil for growing crops is overwhelming. It was cold all night, but daylight brought heat and humidity.

"Where are we again?"

"Missouri."

"Oh. There's nothing here. Why did Papa move here?"

But the trees; never have we seen so many trees. Every direction: trees for miles on the horizon. It is a place of aliveness and solitude.

Traveling from Ohio to Missouri on the train, I was again in awe about the open land. I could never dream there was so much land with no people. We could see ancient primitive people who Americans call Indians. They tried to chase the train once. They wear very little clothing, or animal skins when it is cold. Papa said we should not get off the train in rural areas because of savages. People say they are mean, vicious people who will kill. The Americans want to kill them, and I am uncertain why. If America is the

Land of the Free and they welcome people like me, why do they not welcome the people who have lived here for centuries? Perhaps this New World is just as confusing as Italy; a world caught up in emotions and dreams, but of different natures.

Antonio

We meet Francesco Basile, a good, kind man who helped me gain passage to America. He is a leader among the Italian people in Kansas City, and serves as a liaison to the Italian government. He will help me get a job at an operatic company here. Kansas City is a very small city, on a river called the Missouri River. Francesco tells us that *missouri* is an Indian term meaning "people of the canoes," and I wonder whether there are gondolas along the river like in Venice.

Francesco, or Frank, as he calls himself now, is a tall, well-mannered man with opaque green eyes and light-colored hair. He was born in a small Italian village on the Swiss border. He is considered wealthy, and one of the first, if not the first, person to own a bank in Kansas City, Banca Basile. He hires Italian immigrants to work on the railroad, and also owns a food store, a haberdashery and carpet store. He greets us kindly, somewhat paternally, and inquires about our voyage, our experience at Castle Garden, and our first impressions of America. He has secured performances for us at the Gillis Opera House in Kansas City, and Pietro, Antonio, and Salvatore can perform with me; I am relieved.

While in his parlor, Francesco asks if we may speak alone. I dismiss my sons and daughters. Frank offers me a cigar and sits on a divan close to a window. The winter air is refreshing, not bracing as it often is here in America. We reflect on how life is different here than in the homeland, the politics and political repression in Italy, and the quiet way of life in the Midwest. Francesco says he enjoys his work. Indeed, he has the countenance of a respected man. Corruption, though, is coming to America, even St. Louis and Kansas City, as gangs of Italians try to wield power. One of his primary duties is to make sure Italian men have wives in America, and to make sure Italians are paid for their work. Since the abolishment of slavery, Italians have unfortunately replaced Negroes as slave labor.

"Would you like me to send a telegram, requesting a woman come from your hometown, Naples, to be your wife in America?"

"I have no desire for a wife at this time...I thought I would want to remarry, but..."

"Is there anything else I can do for you?"

"I left my baton in Naples. Oh, it would be so hard to find it. It belonged to my father. Could you help me with that? I am a bit superstitious and fear that losing it may be a bad omen."

"Is it something that would travel well by ship? The voyage is hard on men, women, and objects, as you well know."

"I would rather have it broken and in disrepair than to never lay my eyes on it again."

"Please give me the person to contact in Naples, and I shall send a letter for you on my official stationery as Italian Consulate. Are you sure, Antonio, you do not want a nice young wife to deliver that baton to you? It would be lovely for you to look forward to a wife *and* a baton..."

"No. Perhaps I am unusual, but I do not have any desire for marriage. Letizia is still in my heart."

"When my wife died during childbirth, I found that marrying again helped mend my heart."

"I shall consider the matter."

I walk back into Frank's parlor and find my sons joking about Signor Basile.

"Banca Basile?" one says, giggling.

The other says, "If I were an Italian fella and owned a bank in America and my name were Frank, I would call it Banca Franca."

Then the other son says, "Or Franca Banca."

ELEVEN MONTHS LATER

We have settled into life in Kansas City. My sons have been touring as guest musicians around America. Next week, Pietro and my other sons will perform in Denver; word of their exceptional musical talent while performing here at the Gillis Opera House got all the way out west. They will be traveling there tomorrow, leaving on the afternoon train from Union Station, which is quite grand and the most beautiful train station I have ever seen.

I cannot go with them; Orsola, my oldest daughter, married about ten months ago, to Dominic D'Angelo, and she is expecting her first child in a month, and I want to be here for the blessed event.

Her husband, Dominic, is a fine young man, quite friendly and witty, and I suspect he and Orsola are happy together. He sells rabbits, vegetables, and fruit at the City Market, a new marketplace in the center of the city, on the Missouri River. Life as an immigrant is hard work, and he works thirteen-hour days, but his friendliness wins over the customers, most of whom are women, and this keeps his daily life pleasant, I suspect.

Pietro

Sal, Tony, and I board the train for Denver. They say Denver is more remote than Kansas City, which I cannot imagine. There are Indian people who will scalp you, they say. But Francesco Basile and other people assure us the trip is worth it; there are beautiful mountains, gentle rolling hills, and plenty of cheap land, but the train trip to get there is flat and boring, and the journey is nearly always uneventful. Orsola gives us spaghetti to eat for the first meal, but after that we have only apples, cheese, and bread.

We perform at the Orpheum Theatre, and there is much applause and standing ovations. Afterward, the proprietor offers us a contract for a year. We like Denver, and without much thought, agree on the spot.

Part of the reason why we agree so quickly is that the people of Denver put us up in very nice accommodations, the Brown Palace Hotel; a new, ten-story grand building in the heart of downtown. Everyone is very nice to us, and the crystal clear air and those purple mountains in the distance seem to call to me, more than the monotony of the plains of Kansas and Missouri. The distant mountains remind me of Naples, and my heart hears a call that this shall be home.

When we arrive back at the Brown Palace, a porter walks up to me at a clipped pace. "Maestro! Maestro!" he calls after me. "I have a telegram for you, all the way from Kansas City." My heart sinks and my mind thinks of all kinds of things. I have never received a telegram before. Sal and Antonio gather around and we read:

20 August 1888

Last night I became a grandfather STOP
Orsola and baby are fine STOP
He is named after you, Pietro, Pietro Antonio D'Angelo born 19
    August STOP

We return to Kansas City to visit our new nephew, who will be called Peter, and gather our few belongings. We tell Papa we have decided to move to Denver. He says he no longer has the desire to go to California, where he originally planned to settle; he has an invitation to teach at the University of San Francisco, but thinks he is too old to continue a vagabond life and start anew, and all of his children are starting their lives here. Kansas City and Denver are fine places to live. There is a Jesuit college in Denver, but there is not yet one in Kansas City. He is unsure whether he will come to Denver, but could always take the train to visit; it is a day's journey.

We shall depart in a few weeks, after Peter is baptized.

Peter's baptism is taking place today at St. John's Church, the same church where Orsola and Dominic were married a year ago. He is my namesake, but I pay more attention to girls than I do to babies. I have tried to take an interest in my little nephew, but it is hard. Orsola and Papa have asked me to be the child's godfather, and they tell me this is a special honor. Another musician in the family, we all comment as we sit around the table at Orsola's home at 560 Holmes in Kansas City. It is decided that since Papa plays piano, organ, trumpet, and cornet, and I, too, play all of those instruments, in addition to violin, and Sal plays tuba and Antonio plays clarinet and drums, Peter should be a trombonist. "We will teach him how to buzz as soon as he can walk," my brothers and I joke.

A huge thunderstorm erupts; a common occurrence in Kansas City, I have found. The chandeliers sway, and everything seems very intense. Orsola looks pensive and says more than once, "I will see to it that he is a musician." With each clap of thunder, she grows more adamant, pointing her finger in the air. "*I will see to it that he is a musician.*" She seems to be reassuring Papa and herself that she will keep the musical lines going.

We go to the church all dressed up. It is a cool autumn day. Orsola and her husband Dominic hold baby Peter while the priest, dressed in full robes, speaks in Latin. Then, the baby is handed to me, and the priest anoints him with holy water. I sign his baptismal certificate, P. Satriano.

I really did not know births and christenings were such festive occasions, but the priest and neighbors come to the house, and we all have wine and spaghetti. Papa and my brothers and I play some oratorios, "Ave Maria" and "The Lord's Prayer." Orsola will be a good mother, and will probably have many children, but I am unsure whether I will be a good godfather. A godfather is supposed to lead one spiritually through the Catholic faith. When Mama was alive we went to church frequently but mostly because I was often performing.

Like Papa, music is my theology.

Antonio 1889

I move to Denver to perform with my sons about a year after they arrived here. We all reside together in small houses along the Platte River. We move every year, because the landlord raises the rent. We are saving money, though, and hope to buy a house soon, so we can be the landlords rather than the renters.

I just started teaching at the College of the Sacred Heart. It is a small campus on the western edge of Denver. The college was first located in New Mexico, a small territory to the south. Then it was moved to Morrison, a small town west of Denver, where there are beguiling rock formations with amazing acoustics, better than the opera houses here or in Italy. The college then moved again, to the edge of Denver, because it was a little too remote in Morrison. I ride the trolley to the college from my home; it is the last stop before there is nothing but open land and mountains for hundreds and hundreds of miles, until one gets all the way to Salt Lake City, really.

I have caused my sons to lose some performance contracts. Me, the great opera and waltz composer of Italy, and my drunkenness is starting to permeate everything since moving to America. I cannot stay away from vino and gin. Orsola and her husband, Dominic, did not like my drinking either, and that is partly why I left Kansas City.

One time my sons and I performed at the Tabor Opera House in Leadville. I had my usual four or five drinks before the performance, not a lot really. We really needed the work. My sons were cross with me for drinking before an important performance. It may have been the high altitude there, rumored to be ten thousand feet. I vomited into the bell of my cornet during "Sleeper's Wake." At the time, I thought I was being mindful by vomiting into the cornet rather than on the floor or on my clothing. My sons had to stop playing, and the proprietor came out and said rather curtly, "Thank you, gentlemen, that will be all." We cleaned up the vomit, and I felt ashamed and disgusted with myself. Pietro, always feisty, tried to persuade the man, "Please, please, let us continue. He has been ill lately." The proprietor, a slim, frail, pale man who resembled a ghost, looked disgusted, shook his head in dismay, and sat down again to listen to us, but we still did not get the contract, needless to say.

Pietro came to my office at the college today. He comes to visit, and we play cornet and practice, just like we have done since he was four. We talk about his Mama, Italy, and life in Denver, especially how hard it is to get good *caffe* here. I try to describe the taste, the aroma of good *caffe* in Italia to the other immigrants here, and they do not understand. Pietro knows the other true flavors of Italy from his mother's and sisters' cooking, but we will never again have a good espresso, of which I greatly lament.

My son could have been performing at La Scala, or one of the great cathedrals, and instead he is here, with the cowboys and Indians. He has become a cowboy, riding his horse through town, whipping his horse into a full gallop on the main streets to get attention from the ladies, I believe. In many ways it is a rough life here, rougher than in Italy, but more perplexingly calm also.

Pietro

I married Mae Harrison shortly after arriving here, in what some people still call Denver City, its original name. We married too quickly, and the marriage did not last. I do not like to think about what went wrong, and do not discuss it. Papa is not happy that I divorced; he is concerned about our reputation here in Denver City. I wish Mae well.

My brothers are out courting their betrothed ladies, and Papa stayed at the college last night, so it is a rare time that I get to be alone. I lie in bed and listen to rain drumming on our tin roof. The rain sounds like an angry timpani player beating away. It sounds like the persistent percussion one would find in a marching band, which eventually fades to a soft patter, then crescendos again into percussive, staccato hail pellets, then a ritardando to pianissimo.

Chopin's "Raindrops" is going through my mind; all the great music created on a different continent, and here I am trying to educate people so that great music will also be created on this continent.

Ragtime captures my imagination; the unusual rhythm and beat, some people call it coon music. I love the dances that go with it. I get the most applause from doing the cakewalk and a two-step. Some people think it is inappropriate for a white man to do these things. I do them anyway. Being avant-garde is one of the ways to attain success in America, I believe.

I am a small man. People from other parts of Europe are taller than Italians, I have noticed since living in America. The newspapers sometimes refer to me as "The Little Musician," which I do not really like. Nonetheless, I am petite. I am told I am attractive, and my mother and my ex-wife, Mae, told me I am cute. Papa is a handsome man, very distinguished-looking. In many ways, I wish I, too, were distinguished-looking rather than cute. My hair is black and curly. I part it in the middle and try to keep it tame. It is so thick and curly that I look like a madman if I do not tend to it every day. In keeping with modern times, I do not have a mustache or a beard, as is the custom now, especially with younger men. They say it is not just a fashion, but it is keeping with current scientific thought, germ theory, I believe it is called: invisible things like animals make us sick, and facial hair harbors these creatures that can make us ill.

Adventures of Pinocchio is my favorite book. In many ways his life parallels mine. He mostly wanted to have fun, and lacked morals. He ventured out into an unknown world and got himself into unusual situations; this all sounds like me. I loved reading it. It is the best book ever, and it was one of the few books I brought with me to America. So many of the stories sound like what I have gone through. In the end, Pinocchio changes and learns how to earn a living like his father wants him to. It seems I am following a similar path as Pinocchio now, but who knows what the future holds?

Although I am still young, in my twenties, I notice my nose getting larger, especially longer, as I age. I have certainly told a few high tales in my life, so this could be why. My hands are a bit large for my size, but this is an asset for a musician. My body stays slim, but more and more I take the streetcar, and I notice some weight gain. When I tell people I am gaining weight, they look perplexed and joke, "Which leg has gained a gram, Signor Satriano?"

Life seems to go along smoothly for a while here in the Italian part of the city, where there are small brick and wood-framed bungalows. The soil is reasonably good for growing vegetables. Many of the men who live in the Italian neighborhood work for the railroad, and Frank Basile helped them get jobs. I see them going to work every morning, and think that could be me, if it were not for my musical training. It is said that eighty-five percent of Italian immigrants are unskilled laborers. This puts my family in the fifteen percent range, apparently, but as a musician, sometimes I worry that I could break my fingers, or lose my hearing, or the City Council could decide to bring in a new bandmaster, and then it could easily be me going to work on the railroad. Most of the women here do not know English, and they really do not need to; virtually everyone in the Little Italy section of town speaks Italian.

There is a true sense of community and belongingness here at the base of the Rocky Mountains, in a land so far away from whence we came.

CHAPTER SEVEN

"When Satriano starts the strains of 'The Holy City,'
people are warned something could happen."

Pietro

They come on horseback, they come on foot, on the streetcar, they come with bicycles, and there are starting to be a few motorcars. When we perform at parks, some people get in their boats and listen from the water, because the water amplifies the sound. Most people are dressed up—the men in their suits and top hats and overcoats, the women with their broad hats and long dresses, sometimes carrying parasols. Children come dirty and barefoot. Some boys attend in suits, and some of the girls wear dresses and ribbons in their hair. Men come directly from the slaughterhouse after working twelve-hour days, blood caked to their overalls. Men come with grease on their hands and clothes. Regardless; they come to relax, lovers hoping that music will serve as an elixir to increase their emotions. Parents come with their children or to get away from their children; businessmen come to be seen. Families come with picnic baskets. Old people come to feel alive again; young people come to dream about their futures; women come to talk to other women and show off their fancy dresses. On hot evenings, people come to cool off and wait anxiously for the sun to set over the mountains to the west and await the ensuing onset of the cool evening air that follows. Folks with family visiting bring them to see The Great Satriano Band. People who live across the street walk; people from Colorado Springs come on the train, then walk to the park, or take a carriage ride to the park. On warm evenings, children and lovers swim in the lake. Always, there is a sense of anticipation, a sense of leisure and of fun, and wonderment. Will Satriano do the cakewalk tonight? Will he leap in the air? Will he get angry and will that be the main part of the show, again?

I am a very happy, very busy musician. It is not unusual for me to have two or three performances a day. The people of Denver love music. Elitch Gardens, Lakeside, the Orpheum, the Tabor Opera House, the Chautauqua's in Boulder and Palmer Lake and occasional special performances for Presidents, competitions in other states and inaugurations. Sometimes I go to Colorado Springs to perform at the Broadmoor Hotel or the Antler's Hotel, and my band and I participate in parades. I recently composed the music to coincide with the picture show of the Georgetown train, and I write songs for the high schools in Denver. There is always pressure, always pressure, but I love it. My primary duties, though, have been conducting and playing cornet at Elitch Gardens or with the Denver Municipal Band. We mostly perform at the parks on summer weekends.

We are performing today at Lakeside, known as the Coney Island of the west. It is our first real show with Papa, Tony, Sal and me. I am hoping to prove that we are the finest musicians in Denver. The show will start at 8:00 p.m. tonight and it is 6:00 p.m. now. Tony and Sal complained about practicing so long; they think we would be better off practicing for an hour and then we will sound fresh at performance time. I can see Sal in the distance now. Sal is a large man, about four to five inches taller than my brothers and me. They say when he was born he weighed eight pounds, and Papa joked there would finally be a tuba player in the family! Sal lumbers along in a slow, easy manner, a lot like the bears we sometimes see walking downtown. They come down from the mountains to eat rubbish. Sal is quiet but often smiling; it gives him an air of confidence.

"I just saw Papa. He is drunk. Too much gin. I don't know whether he will be able to play," Sal says.

"His drinking is getting worse. We need to tell him *basta!* But the paradox is, the more inebriated he is, the better he composes."

"How can we stop him?" Sal says rhetorically.

"It started when we got to America. He must be unhappy here."

"Are you happy here?" Sal looks at me intently.

I did not know how to answer. "Music first, always," I mutter.

"Let's go get Papa. We'll give him some *caffe.*"

Just then, we see Papa, outside without his hat on, his shirt indecently exposing his chest. His topcoat is dirty, and I can smell the gin this far away. He is disheveled, very flush. Not the Papa I used to know. This is the Papa he became.

"Papa, you must stop. You cannot continue to drink this way. You will ruin our reputation in Denver and your health! Basta!"

He sits in a wooden chair under a tree. He is unshaven and looks like a squatter rather than an eminent musician.

"It tears my heart to see you doing this, Papa. This is not the man you are." I grab him by his lapel and shake him, partly to emphasize my point, but partly to keep him from passing out.

Papa stands up. He has tears in his eyes and tries to take a swing at Sal, but his hook is weak and extending his arm causes him to lose balance and fall. Lying on the ground, he says something in Italian; what it is, I am not sure, but the ladies at the Catholic church would be quite appalled at what he likely said.

"Where is your trumpet, Papa?" Sal asks.

"I sold it."

We both say in unison, "Why?"

He just stares at us with tears in his eyes.

"We have to do a show tonight. Sal, how much money do you have?"

Sal is looking through his pockets, counting coins. I, too, get out the coins in my pockets. Between the two of us, we have $3.50.

"Go get Tony, tell him we need to buy a trumpet for Papa. With this money, we should have enough to buy a used one from Knight-Campbell's." I lower my voice and move in closer to Sal. "Explain to them about Papa, maybe they will have sympathy and reduce the price." I slap the money in his hand and say, "Go!"

Sal wastes no time. He jumps on his horse, gives the horse a swift kick, grabs the reins with his left hand, and simultaneously puts his hat on with his right hand.

Papa gets off count several times. I give him a few icy glances. He knows when I'm looking at him, but whether he knows my anger is about poor musicianship and being tired of his drunkenness, I am not sure. He seems to sober up a lot when he performs, as if the music is an antidote to his poison, booze.

After the performance, Papa starts to walk away with his new cornet. So drunk, he does not inquire where it came from or to whom it belongs. When told we bought it for him, he does not thank us for purchasing a new one.

I stop him. "We cannot let you take this with you. You will sell it." He grips it tighter and holds it to his chest.

"But I need it," he says with great conviction, trembling.

"You only think you need it!" I rise from my chair, yelling. He is like a child sometimes. How does one get through to a drunken child?

Sal comes up behind him and holds him. Papa's worn body looks childlike next to Sal's.

I grab his cornet and again he mutters something in Italian; "Vino and gin, that is all there is anymore. Without that, I am no one."

I am too upset with Papa and leave him there to mutter to himself. Sal and I meet up with Tony, who is standing outside waiting, and we ride together.

My brothers and I discuss how we are going to hide the cornet. We all ride our horses home slowly. Before heading for our small house, we let the horses have a long drink from the Platte River. The stars are beautiful at night in Denver. On this night, there is a full moon, so the stars are playing second violin and the moon is the main attraction. We can see the ground well because the moon's light is mimicking the sun's rays. Our horses seem to prance along happily. Nighttime in Denver is spectacular; the thin air and high altitude allow the stars and moon to shine brightly. Daytime abandons those stars, but they reappear every night for a repeat performance, an encore over the Rocky Mountains that supersedes that of any orchestra.

We reach our house and wander to the garden patch. We sit mesmerized by the stars, and everything is peaceful, except for the problem with Papa. We have discussed the problem with him time and again, to no avail.

We know what we have to do without speaking the words. Sal goes around to different homesteads along the river and asks for shovels.

He returns with three shovels, and we all start digging deep holes in our vegetable garden by the light of the moon. We dig to about three feet, put Papa's new cornet into the ground, and cover the hole.

I say, "I never thought it would come to this. I have never heard of anyone having to do this."

We stand there looking at the ground, and the newly dug-up earth that looks like a gravesite, which, in a way, it is.

Papa continues to be drunk every night, except Sundays. He is often incoherent. Tony talks to Father Lepore about Papa's drinking, and he says there are doctors starting to specialize in this problem, and we should take him to a doctor.

CHAPTER EIGHT

"…A combination of excellence and celebrated
aggregations of musical talent in (this family) line."

Pietro

I will never forget that first time I saw her in Denver, apparently just a few days after she arrived in Colorado. I was walking to the Tabor Opera House for an evening performance and thought I saw an attractive lady in the distance, walking among people strolling along Curtis Street, talking and going to the concerts and picture shows. I quickened my step, afraid I would lose her. I did not think it was Anna, I thought it was a girl who looked like Anna. The women and their large hats these days; it is impossible to see around them, and even if one can, the hats obscure their faces.

For a while I thought I lost her. It reminded me of how I would sneak around in the old auditorium, night after night, waiting to get a glimpse of Anna. Then suddenly, the crowd cleared and there she was. Anna. I thought I was dreaming. She looked at me with her huge brown eyes wide open and her mouth open as if about to sing a high note in an aria. I could not believe we were both in Denver, so far away from Milan, standing in the middle of a dirt street on a bright Wednesday afternoon.

She looked exactly the same, exotic, her hair long and eyes that remind one of good Swiss chocolate.

We are inseparable for days, and I bring her home for dinner. I tell Papa, Sal, and Antonio about her lovely voice and how we met. She is too shy to sing that first night, but thereafter, she sings in her rich operatic voice after dinner while we all smoke cigars and Papa drinks gin.

After a few months, our fathers go with us to the Arapahoe County Courthouse and sign papers acknowledging that they know she is fifteen and a half, but give their consent for us to marry anyway.

For the most part, that is the end of the good memories. She is a tease, always a tease, a trickster. And, she brings out the wild man in me, I must admit. I was in love with her; her love was intoxicating, and the more she withdrew, the more I wanted her. These days, there are doctors called psychoanalysts, and maybe they would know why her erratic behavior and moodiness made me want her more. Now, the men at the Italian Lodge and men in my band tell me their wives also want them to go to one of these new doctors. I ask the men in my band if they tell their wives to go to one of these doctors, and they say no. I scratch my head about this. They are supposedly the weaker sex, but we should go to the doctors who help people with mind problems?

Her father moved to Boston just a few days after our wedding. He left her here, knowing that Papa and I would take care of her. Papa is especially upset about the situation, and our tempestuous relationship takes even more of a toll on his health, I am afraid. Anna is becoming more childlike, demanding and crying all the time. Trying to control me and arguing, yet trying to be a wife at the same time. When Papa and my brothers complained one too many times, I managed to get us a house of our own and we moved two blocks away. For a while, things were better. She stayed home, and made our new home comfortable. She cooked wonderful spaghetti and I was starting to be happy. But then she would be out late. I would hear rumors she was keeping the company of other men in the Red Light District. Denver society thinks it is outrageous enough that I married such a young girl, and that I cannot keep her at home. Papa worries about the negative publicity that my marriage and my wife's behavior is getting. Divorce is the only answer. We all try to do our best to be a family, but Anna's moods and instability are too much.

I went to jail because she is a wild, aggressive young lady. I must divorce this woman, and I will find a better wife. Still, I will miss her. I will have to become good at avoiding thoughts of her. She is always there, a whisper in my mind.

But let me be clear: I am not a saint myself. She brings out the fiery temper in me. I admit it. We both get mad and fly into rages. We fought so much last night, like lions fighting over one of Mama's meatballs. She makes me so angry. If only she could be a good wife. I know she is still seeing other men.

I am arrested one night and put in the pokey. My lawyer reminds me of Puccini; he definitely overindulges in pasta and his wife must be an excellent cook, for I do not know how else a man could acquire such a large belly.

"Hey, Pete, I talked to the judge. Ah…the news isn't good. You'll have to stay in jail."

I stand up; my rage is equal to what it is when Anna and I fight.

I grasp the cold bars of my cell, "You get me out of here. I am a royal musician. We do not spend time in cow town jails!" I rattle the bars, I have never been so angry. "My wife is out of control, and I am in here? I am The Great Satriano…you do something…now!"

Barrister Teasdale, I believe that is his name, walks backward in shock. He grabs his enormous belly, and says with clenched teeth that have bits of food in them, "Young man, control yourself. You may have a hussy of a wife on your hands, but do not get yourself further in trouble by threatening me."

And with that, he turns on one foot, his rotund body shifting accordingly, and waddles away.

In jail, I compose a letter to my friend, Puccini. We knew each other at the Royal Academy of Music in Milan. I have been meaning to write to him for some time.

Dear Maestro Puccini,

I hope this letter finds you and your family well.

I miss our days of frolic at the conservatory in Milan. Your music reflects your humor, and I am writing to tell you that one of your opera songs, "Mio Bambino Caro," actually happened in my life recently.

While in Milan, as you may know, I fell in love with a very young girl, Anna, who had the softest, sweetest voice I ever heard. I did not think I would ever see her again, but the strangest thing happened: she moved to where I live, to Denver, Colorado in the United States. I could not control myself and she was quite flirtatious. Then her father decided he was going to move to a different state, and Anna did not want to move because she did not want to leave me, supposedly. One thing led to another, and she convinced her father that she should stay here and be my wife. Then, I learned that she was only fifteen and a half. Her father relented, but only because she said she was pregnant with my child, which was untrue. She would whine and cry, "Oh, Daddy please!" just like the character in your opera. She threatened to jump off the tallest building in Denver (we do not really have any bridges here, to speak of).

Your song, known as the Italian *Romeo and Juliet*, my fella, came alive for me. I curse you. She never did have a baby and she made a fool of me in this fine city. Did you send this woman all the way to America to haunt me? Is it a cruel joke, Signor Puccini?

I am somewhat facetious, of course, my friend.

Speaking of facetiousness, you would not believe the article that appeared in a Denver paper. According to a scientist, if our dear friend, opera singer Enrico Caruso, sang an unspecified note for a long time, the vibrancy of it could break his bones, and cause him to disintegrate or could render him into a "jellyfish-like mass."

I have been laughing, literally laughing, about this for days. The newspapers here are quite funny.

Yours truly,

Pietro Satriano, Musical Director, Elitch Gardens

Denver, Colorado, United States of America

COURTROOM, ONE WEEK LATER

The room is all wood, and rather new. There are so many new buildings in America compared to Italy. The candles along the walls are lit, and sun streams through the only window facing east.

The judge has attended my concerts many times, and I have dined with him at the mayor's home more than once. He loves whiskey and likes to smoke a corn pipe. I am thinking about how he might view me very favorably, when suddenly I hear loudly, "All rise!" Mr. Teasdale, my rotund attorney, who reminds me not only of Puccini, but also of a gigantic tuba or a full-size string bass, shakes me so that I can rise and abide the proper decorum. While we stand to acknowledge Judge Wain's presence in the courtroom, Mr. Teasdale whispers to me, "Lots of people are here today because of you. Be on your best behavior. The public wants to see you act respectfully. This is not a show."

Just like the time all those years ago, when Orsola told me not to visit the psychic lady or when I was told to sit quietly and practice chords for hours, I suddenly want to scream, dance, play "Holy City" on my cornet, and run like a madman. But this time, I tell myself, I must behave.

I take the stand. When the deputy calls my name, all eyes are on me. I love this, it is like performing. There are muted whispers and then absolute silence. It is just like when I enter the band shell to perform. I put my hand on the *Bible* and prepare to tell the truth, the whole truth and nothing but the truth, so help me God. But is there really a God? I think there is not.

I think of ancient times, when men held their manhood rather than placing their hand on the *Bible*. The words testimony and testify are derived from this ritual. The voice of reason is adamantly telling the entertainer side of me not to do that…

My lawyer begins. "Professor Satriano, where were you when you were arrested?"

"I was conducting my band at the Orpheum Theatre. We were performing Othello."

"You were in the middle of the performance?"

"Si, I was, yes."

Gasps from all over the courtroom.

Papa is generally regarded as one of the composers who did the best re-interpretation of Verdi's "Othello." We were halfway through the show, and in walked two policemen. They had their clubs out and were looking me in the eye. I kept the musicians playing as long as possible. The policemen became impatient and walked onto the stage. My men stopped playing. "Signor Satriano, I am sorry, but the judge said to come and arrest you. He is afraid you will skip town."

The audience started booing. My men said, "Leave him alone. His wife is the problem…Just let us finish!" I told them my old spiel, about how once a musician starts, he or she cannot be interrupted under any circumstances. They looked at me for a second; with no pity, they threw my baton to the ground. The audience booed even more, and some people threw cups, handkerchiefs, and scarves onto the stage.

"Let the maestro do his work!"

"Leave the Little Italian guy alone!"

"A man has the right to work!"

"Down in front! I can't see. We are in the middle of an aria… please!"

I left the stage that night in the most dramatic way ever. I loved it. The people applauded. Life is so strange sometimes. And so different than it is in our dreams.

"And why were you arrested?" the judge asks, interrupting my thoughts.

"My wife is out of control. My wife is guilty of diverse and sundry acts unbecoming a devoted wife."

There is absolute silence now. Only the wooden benches creak a little.

"Can you give the court some examples of her behavior, other than her indecent behavior?"

"She has broken no less than eight pairs of my spectacles."

Gasps from the audience. Everyone turns their eyes toward Anna.

The judge looks at me directly and says, "There are certainly worse things a wife could do. Why such rowdiness on your part because she does this?"

"Unfortunately, all the spectacles were perched on my nose at the time."

The judge, my attorney, and all the spectators laugh. The judge has a wonderful guffaw, and after a few seconds, he regains his dignity, pounds the gavel a few times, and says, "Order in the court! Order in the court!"

My attorney, Mr. Teasdale, whispers to me, "It is as important to be as brilliant in your mistakes as it is in your brilliance."

The judge tells me I can get down from the stand. My attorney asks him whether I can be released, as I need to return to work; I have another performance at the Orpheum Theatre. The judge reluctantly says I can go, but he gives me a stern warning, "Stay out of trouble, young man."

Burying our instruments in the garden was working well; Papa has not found our hiding place. It is extra work for us, however. Almost every day we have to dig them up and clean them because we have rehearsals or performances, and then we have to bury them again at night. Then, one night Tony was too tired to bury his clarinet and Papa found it. Tony awakened in the wee hours of morning to find Papa drunk, walking out the door with it, probably going to the bar at the corner of Fifteenth and Platte to trade it for money to buy gin. He also sold Mama's wedding ring and her good silver. We have extra performances scheduled so that we can buy them back.

But somehow today, my brothers and I have convinced Papa to see a doctor about his drinking. He never drank like this before we came to Colorado. Papa looks frail. He is shaking and seems frightened, but is also uncharacteristically angry and short tempered. "I am fine, I am fine…" he keeps saying as we walk him to the doctor's office.

The doctor does not have much to say. He tells Papa he is drinking too much and his liver is enlarged.

"Professor Satriano, you have dipsomania, an overpowering desire for intoxication."

Papa looks down, shaking. He did not have a glass of vino or gin this morning; he was trying not to go to the doctor while intoxicated, and trying to prove to us he does not need it, but abstaining causes him to shake more.

"Why do you drink?" the doctor asks.

Papa does not answer.

"Immigrants are especially vulnerable. The intense pressures… the dreams of a better life thwarted by work, prejudice, the same problems here as in Italy, in some ways, no?" the doctor says, trying to get him to talk.

"Si. I am a weak man. A dreamer who lost the dream…"

"No, you are a man who has a medical problem. Here is some cocaine; it is a rather new treatment, and some people find it helpful. Just use a small amount, and you will likely notice your desire for alcohol decreasing. If this does not help, there is a new hospital for this problem, what the common people call the 'Jitter Joint.' Think about it."

Papa seems intrigued with this white substance, sometimes thought to be a magical cure because it could help alleviate desire for booze and cure other ailments. When we leave, he shakes hands with the doctor and sincerely thanks him, and he walks home with a bit more confidence.

We part ways, and I walk toward the Orpheum Theatre for rehearsal. It is warm, and the gentle autumn days are a tease for the harshness of winter and the snow that will soon be upon us. The restaurants and bars have the windows open, to let in some of the last warmth before the autumnal snows begin.

As I walk along at a brisk pace, I hear my name from the ruckus of a tavern.

"Signor Satriano said…"

"He never really…"

The streetcar goes by, and with the noise of dishes clattering, I cannot quite get every word at times. I stop to listen, and position myself where no one who is talking can see me. I light a cigar and listen to the conversation, pretending like I just happen to be standing on Sixteenth Street, passing time.

"The Little Musician," one says, "in court complaining his wife beats him!"

"What kind of a man would admit to the public that his wife beats him? He must be cowardly."

"I think he is brave to admit it. He is small, you know."

"Ah, but so is she."

"Touché, true, true. Those little women can be menacing, you know."

"And so could a little man."

"Maybe Signor Satriano is making the whole thing up, maybe he is just looking for an excuse to divorce her, because she is a woman of ill repute…will lift her petticoat to any man who happens by."

"It is just a rumor she is that kind of lady…"

"I think she is a sweet girl devastated because her father left her, and she has no mother…and she is in this new place, trying to be a wife, and so young. Have sympathy for the child," says the older woman.

"Si, he must be embarrassed. Can't keep a wife happy. First Mae, now Anna…"

"Those are merely rumors. We don't know for sure," chimes another voice, with a great clinking of glasses.

"His temper, momma mia! Maybe he is the one breaking *her* spectacles."

"Just because he is publically fiery does not mean he is privately."

"The newspapers sometimes call Signor Satriano 'The Young Man with Glasses.' They should start calling him 'The Young Man *Without* Glasses,' apparently!" Everyone laughs, takes a swig of gin or beer or whatever is close at hand.

"Divorces are rare…who divorces? No one. It is a sin."

"Si, but the Satrianos' are also rare. Who has that much talent? To come to America when they had it so good there…"

The people shake their heads in unison, and then are quiet. I imagine they are pondering this.

A lady starts to speak, "I want to tell you something about Signor Satriano…"

But several horse drawn carriages go by, and I miss what she says.

"…Well, he certainly is entertaining," says the lady wearing a large hat, what society and the newspapers refer to as an *aggressive hat*. She looks down, focuses on her sherry and seems to feel her statement has made an impact.

"The way his body sways to the music. His dancing. My, it is obscene, obscene I tell you! Indecent." The lady pounding her fists on the table.

Another lady, whom I like very much, says "I rather like the way his lithe body moves" she giggles. "They all do it now-Sousa, Bellestedt. They all want to be the people's favorite and go to great lengths to surprise us. They have to be different, how else would they get people to attend performances?"

I walk away quickly, amused to have had this brief glimpse into what people are saying about me on the street.

CHAPTER NINE

"Twenty-three thousand people
at park to hear Satriano's Band"

Antonio

C ontrary to what my sons may say, I remain sober during the day for my professional duties at the college. Always.

I have been happy teaching at College of the Sacred Heart, and I started an orchestra and a band here. It is good that the college values Italians and they have recruited us to be on its faculty. I did feel slighted, however, when the college failed to acknowledge that I was the composer of a song we performed recently, "A Hero's Grave." They did rectify the situation, however, in the college's newspaper, *The Highlander*, of March 1891, said that through benign inadvertence during the ceremony, it was not mentioned that "The Hero's Grave" was written by me.

Currently, I am with a student, a young Mr. Tydings, who moved here from England. Mr. Tydings is a quiet, nervous young man who is very fair skinned and has a slight lisp. Behind this awkwardness, though, he has the potential to shine as a musician. He is in his first year of studies at College of the Sacred Heart, but he just completed taking Music Theory with me, and plays the violin with great will.

By his nervousness, I am wondering whether he has come to talk to me about a personal matter. Sometimes students confide in their professors concerns about the young lady they are courting, or missing their families, or other family matters. My job as a professor allows me to give fatherly advice all day. But I am wrong: he is not here to discuss these types of issues.

"Professor Satriano…I have a concern that may be…a rather unusual concern…" He blushes.

Ah, he wants to know about relations between men and women, I think.

"I am afraid that if I study music, it will…lose its appeal… music is mysterious. If I learn too much about the science of it…"

"Mr. Tydings, I assure you, the formal study of music will not strip you of your enjoyment, it will be heightened. I really do not think one's ability to enjoy music is diminished by analytical knowledge. It may deepen appreciation for the mystery of music."

He looks relieved. His shoulders relax and his face becomes less red.

"It was on my mind also, when I was a young man starting out. Other students have come to me with similar concerns, here and in Italy."

He looks at me for a long time, clears his throat, and looks away and says, "Thank you, sir."

He puts on his hat quickly, smiles, thanks me again, and leaves. I think I alleviated his fears, and hope I told him what he wanted to hear. I will be curious as to whether he will continue in music. Studying music is all consuming, all encompassing, or at least it should be.

I try to resume my lesson planning, and then Pietro comes to the door. We greet each other the Italian way, an embrace and a kiss on each cheek. Pietro seems energetic and young, but also always restless, like his Papa. He is not happy with his young wife, Anna, and rumors about our family abound in Denver City. He is on his way to play music in the mountains at what we call our natural opera house near here, where beautiful cliffs act as soundboards: Garden of the Titans.

I tell him about the challenges I face as a music professor. He looks at me and says, "Papa, any time you play music you are teaching people about music."

"I do not think the public wants to be taught," I add. My son, pedantic even with his Papa.

Pietro got interested in a music form called ragtime when we were in Kansas City. *Mama mia!* The music young people like today. I tell him he should remain in the family tradition as a classicist; the classics will never go away. He says all music is good. I tell him to be careful, that it is the music of Africa, and that people here despise the Africans. Many people of Germanic and British heritage hate Italians as much as the Negro people, and many people in America think Italians are Negro people. I worry that Pietro's reputation could be harmed by playing that music. He listens to a Negro man, Scott Joplin, play a song called "The Entertainer" over and over on his gramophone. It sounds like wild Africa music to me. The piano sound is raw, and is syncopated with a ragged rhythm. My other son, Tony, likes it too and plays the drums in a wild manner. I worry my sons will be discriminated against by their choice of this music. The children do not always listen to their Papa, and for this reason I worry. We have dark skin and hair, and Pietro's hair is a bit curly. What if he is not accepted into the music community here in Colorado?

I express my concerns to him, and he counters, "*You* are hurting our reputation in Denver, you and your drinking." He is right, I cannot stop.

"Italians are being hanged in Colorado, and many other states."

"Si; I know, Papa. I will watch myself. But you must watch yourself, too."

"Why do they dislike us so? Because our skin is dark? We have given them beautiful art, music, food, architecture and hard labor.

I was not expecting…they revere us in so many ways, yet despise us in so many other ways…And, the way Americans treat the people from Africa! I love the people from Africa. They may have abolished slavery in America, but they did not abolish their barbaric behavior or attitudes toward people they deem as undesirable."

Pietro looks at me. I know he is scared; underlying his occasional arrogance is fear. He handles this fear, this subterfuge of prejudice and potential violence, by absorbing himself in music. I, too, do that, but also use the bottle as aid. We have a close community here in Denver, but just because we have many Italians here in Denver colony does not mean we cannot be accused of something we did not do, or given a punishment worse than the crime. I saw a comic strip of an obviously Italian person hanging from a noose on the Statue of Liberty; such a cruel country this is. There are reports that more than ten Italians have been hanged in Colorado alone over the last seven years.

Again, we talk about Garden of the Titans. He sees the native people there sometimes, and is intrigued by their drums and flutes. I should like to go there someday, I have heard colleagues mention this place with great acoustics, similar to the opera houses in Europe. Pietro is young and impressionable; I hope these Indians and this ragtime music do not interfere with his thinking. He is a classicist and should remain a classicist. Why, a Satriano performing African music is preposterous…

I feel melancholic after my discussion with Pietro; children have a way of making their parents feel proud and guilty all at the same time. Perplexing job, this parenting business. It would have been easier for me if Letizia were here.

These ruminations must be put on hold now, as I must go teach my afternoon Brass course.

I walk to my class and the sky is beautiful here above Denver. I may have erred in moving to Colorado, but the sunshine lifts my spirits, even when I miss Letizia, espresso, and *caffe*.

On days like this, when I have a heavy heart, it is more rewarding to teach, and it releases my mind from the worries of the day, and elevates teaching to the level of a sacred act.

I stand in front of my Brass Instruments class. I want to reach the young students, but like all professors, I grapple with how. I want them to feel, see, and breathe the music. Unless they are playing music, they all look bored. Lectures can be meaningless teaching tools when it comes to music. Like me, their hearts and spirits want to soar. They know if they can make the hearts and spirits of others soar, they will be able to earn a living as musicians. What can I do to make their dreams come true? All I can do is play for them, help them improve, and describe what has been written and studied about music, but again and again, I question: Is it enough?

I begin my lecture: "In Italy, one of my colleagues in the Architecture Department used to say 'trying to write about music would be like trying to dance about architecture.' How can it really be described, or explained, with words? Johann Wolfgang von Goethe said something similar, "music is liquid architecture; architecture is frozen music." It cannot really be done. So I stand before you as a professor of music, limited. I can listen and play music, but beyond that it is a *lingua franca*, a type of currency for people who do not have similar currency; it is a third language. Always remember this. And, now, gentlemen, let us pick up our instruments and play to feel that third language, and see whether we can bring forth angels. Let us call forth the angels; believe it is so. This is what we do for people." The students stand up immediately. I worry that my unusual lecture has them frightened.

I get my baton and add, "Remember, to musicians, the baton means 'go,' but to the audience, the baton means 'show.' " And with that, we begin playing "The Holy City."

"Remember," I say, "we are calling forth the angels..."

Out of nowhere, there appear to be tiny flecks of white flying through the classroom. At first, I think birds have come in through an open window. The students initially look startled, but continue to play. Then they seem to almost take it in stride; we have called forth angels. Are we imagining tiny angels flying through, or are they real? Or some imagined dust particles, merely excited by my enthusiastic lecture? Are they entirely of this world or the world of fantasy?

CHAPTER TEN

"The cortege formed a procession going
from the church to the capitol,
thence to Fairmount."

Pietro November 1899

Tony knocks on my door at about midnight. It is the worst news. "Papa is dying." I am confused; he seemed to be in fine form a few days ago. All I can think to say is, "Are you sure? Get Father Lepore. Where is Salvatore?"

"They are at his side as well. It will not be long…"

"I want to be there with him…when he goes."

We have a funny relationship with the Church. The Church did not look favorably on my divorce, and although we can attend service, they believe I sinned in being divorced, and this affected my whole family. They rejected all of us because of my errors in judgment. Father Lepore was different, though. He is a real character and more liberal than the Church in general. Both Anna and Mae confided in him, and I suspect he has heard quite a bit about me.

I hope Father is going to the heaven he wants to be in. My father is a believer, but his beliefs are vague and unclear to me.

I have to walk a few blocks in blinding snow. The snow looks like small crystals lying on the streets and sidewalks. I pull my hat tighter over my head. The snowflakes are large, and I can't see well. I notice my eyes are moist, but tell myself it is from the snow and not tears because Papa is dying. He is a sentimental man, an emotional man, who likes the emotion in a melodious melody. Papa does not think it is wrong for a man to cry.

The room is dark. At the bedside, there is one lit candle, and Father Lepore is standing over him, giving him the Sacrament of Last Rites. It reminds me so much of the time I had to say goodbye to Professor Romano. The squeaky door, the wooden planks... Papa looks white, his skin looks like pasta, all pasty. He can barely talk. He is imagining Mama is there, I think. He says, "Letizia... Letizia..." over and over. I don't know if he sees her or if she is really with him. He looks at me and says in Italian, "My boy... I am sorry..."

I start to tell him there is no reason for apology, but then realize his eyes are glazy and open unusually wide. His jaw has dropped. He is dead.

I will never know why he was sorry. Sorry for what? He told me he dreamed of Italy in his sleep. Of when life was calm and gentle, of his parents and my mother and the opera that he loved so, La Scala, and being in Venice.

I will never know whether he was sorry for bringing me to America, or whether it was some other reason. One way or another, those were the last words the great composer ever spoke.

To pay tribute to my father, state officials decided on the funeral procession. We start from Mt. Carmel Church, go past the state capitol, and then to Fairmount Cemetery. My brothers and I are among the sixty musicians performing for Papa, all of us members of the Denver Musicians' Protective Association.

I feel like I am here, but at the same time not here. Right now we are playing Chopin's "Funeral March." I have heard this song and performed it on numerous occasions, but now it is being played for Papa. These chords—every one of them—is striking deep, deeper than ever. The heavy, repetitious melody shoots through me like arrows in my veins, as if Chopin wrote this piece just for me, or just for Papa, here in this moment, to forever hold these arrowed veins captive in my soul. Everything about him was musical. I must collect myself and remember that at this time, I am both a musician and a mourner. I am the leader of the band, and the oldest son, and therefore leader of the Satriano family now.

Every note is him. The lead horse has no rider, to signify Papa's loss; and this analogy, this sight, pierces through me more deeply than anything. My brothers always felt slighted, because Papa paid more attention to me than to my brothers. Part of it may have been my name, Pietro. I was named after his father, and he and Papa were very close. If there is a God, which I doubt, but if there is, God will ask him, "Signor Professor Satriano, your music was divine. How did you know what heaven was like before arriving?"

I smile, and Sal sees me smiling and gives me a cold stare to remind me that this is a solemn event, and whatever I am thinking about, it is improper decorum at this time. Then, we begin Beethoven's "Funeral March," which is easier; it does not reach me in the same way. It does not remind me of Papa, and I am relieved. Then I am able to think of it as someone else's funeral, not my beloved Papa's.

I am glad that many people lined the streets to watch my father's last ride, his last performance, as a man and a musician. It is a solemn occasion. I see the mayor and the governor. Most of the musicians in the band have been students of Papa's, and the ones who haven't have been students of mine. The day fortunately is bright and sunny, but the wind howls down from the mountains like an invisible lion's roar, like a witch coming to steal the things you want to hold onto most dearly but cannot see or grasp.

I watch Papa's casket being placed in the earth, here in the middle of nowhere, and thousands of miles from the place from whence he came, from the people who knew him best. How many men have been born in Naples, lived several places in Italy, fought in a civil war with an infamous leader and then lived in New York,

Missouri and Colorado? No one; like many other things, Papa will be the first in the world. And, it is sad. He was looking forward to the year 1900, and wanted to have lived in two different centuries.

At the gravesite, Father Lepore asks if I want to say a few words. I was not expecting this, and suddenly feel shy. Most people probably do not know of my shyness.

I take out my handkerchief, wipe my nose, and look out at all the people at the funeral. Governor Thomas and Mayor Johnson are there, many Italian immigrants we know from our neighborhood, some of his colleagues from College of the Sacred Heart, and Concetta's husband, Frank Russomanno, a great trombonist. I say, "Father was truly an adventurer. He fought in wars and loved the excitement of battle, yet he was also a sentimental man. Paradoxically, he was also a refined man, who performed in many fine opera houses in Europe. He loved his family, especially my Mother, and he wanted what was best for us, and that, ultimately is why we live in America. Grazie, Papa, for inspiring all of us with your love of music and your adventurous spirit."

The men start to throw dirt over the grave. I, too, throw dirt on his grave; this archaic ritual that seems so barbaric; I have always hated this, and it seems demeaning to throw dirt on a loved one's grave. He is gone forever, and now a part of history. Will his work be remembered?

The hand of time seems to wash away so much, I think, as I throw American soil on Papa's grave.

Later, Tony, Sal and I have a gin together, to honor Papa. Concetta is here also, although she does not drink gin. "We lost Papa because of it. Mama would have been very hurt by his drinking," she says as she pours our drinks.

We think he drank so much because of Mama's death, but also the war was unimaginable, and he drank to rid himself of nightmares of death and gore. He was never quite the same, Mama said.

This is a rare occasion for Concetta to get out of the house and spend time with adults, rather than with her young children. I tell them what I really should have said at the gravesite was, "There was no man I tried harder to please, no man who was harder *to* please, and no man who tried harder to please me."

"He was a romantic, sailing the seas, and always, faithfully, religiously, sent money back to us in Avelino Bagnoli after he moved to America. He cared about his family."

We look at the article about Papa in the *Denver Post* entitled, "An Eminent Musician Gone."

Then Concetta stops reading and looks out the window, her eyes tearing, "At least we know Papa and Mama are together now."

We all sit quietly and watch the snow pile up outside. A huge snowstorm has come in from the west, and we may be buried under two feet of snow by morning. It is hard on the horses and cattle when this happens, and some of the immigrants die because there is not enough firewood to go around. Italians are some of the poorest immigrants. The shacks along the river are full, often with five to ten people living in one room; it is always sad when a snowstorm comes. The churches are getting fuller every year, as more and more families move here from Europe and the east, and the poor especially have to rely on the Church.

Without Papa, it is time for Sal, Tony, and me to make it on our own. We have families to feed. There are always new problems in tandem with building a life, and every day brings more problems.

Part Two
1901–1918

CHAPTER ELEVEN

"Signor Satriano should mind his manners"

Pietro

My marriage to Anna ended. Father Lepore annulled it, which many devout Catholics did not approve of, but he liked Papa, and Papa had some sway with him. For some people in the Italian colony, it was one more move that caused Father Lepore to be disliked, and it did not increase my standing in the community either, except among those who follow the gossip columns.

About a year after she moved to Boston to be with her father, Anna married another Italian man. Her father killed himself with morphine, and her second husband left her and returned to Italy a few years after their marriage. Maybe it would have been better if she had stayed here with me and been my wife "in holy matrimony," as the Christians say.

I am just lucky the people of Denver are so forgiving. I married a girl, then divorced, then Papa was a dipsomaniac, and everyone knew, but they overlooked it. Then I married again and divorced. In Italy, this never would have happened. In America, one is free, and I have certainly taken my liberties and gotten the best of this freer world since we arrived on June 16, 1885. In Italy, I would have always been married to Anna, and taken a good deal of ribbing for being unable to keep my young wife happy.

With Father Lepore's annulment, I was free to marry whomever I liked. He admonishes, "Try to find someone your own age!"

"Father, I will, but the young woman had the voice of an angel and the hair of a goddess."

He looks at me and shakes his head. "You're a young man. Let your mind guide your choice, not your heart or lust. You are deserving of a good wife, Pietro, choose a good Christian woman…"

TWO WEEKS LATER

I am sitting at home on a quiet spring evening, and I hear a commotion. People are running through the streets. "Father Lepore has been shot!! The dear Father Lepore shot during a poker game. St. John bless us all!" The bells at Mt. Carmel Church start ringing to get people's attention that there is a crisis, and beckon the believers to come. News spreads through town as fast as a Rocky Mountain wildfire. The news is that beloved Father Lepore is in grave condition, and probably not going to make it. People gather at the church.

They talk and weep. The original church burned down several months ago, and we are in a temporary rectory. It is dark inside; people light candles. "I hear he had a sordid past…business dealings back in Italy. He came all the way here to get as far away from Italy as possible. I do not really know whether he was a man of the cloth… Do you think he was?"

"Yes," another woman replies. "He was a sinner who repented his sins by ministering to our needs." Even people from other Catholic churches come. Mae comes; she enjoyed talking to Father Lepore, though I am afraid their conversations were often about her grievances with me. "Oh, how could it happen to a priest, a man of God? Holy Mary, Mother of God, what is the world coming to?"

Another man chimes in, "It is like being back in Italy during the Civil War!"

"Eh, Lepore was a deceptive man. I am not surprised someone killed him. He was not a priest! He took the sanctity out of the sanctuary. A priest preserves the sanctuary, at all costs. Because of him, our parish's reputation has suffered!" Most people present are speaking in Italian. The voices escalate at times, as if we are at a party, and then hush as people remember we are in church.

Signora Sinatra calls out, "We must remember, we are in a sacred place. Father Lepore is dying or dead, please show respect!" She holds her index finger to her lips, the show of silence. Then, quietly, one lady says in the hushed room, "First the church burned down due to arson, now this." We wonder whether these two events are related.

The taverns keep the candles lit until late for us.

Although we all live in Denver, in our hearts and minds, we seem to live in other places simultaneously. We live in our small homes, the bars, the parks and churches, but we also live in Italy. When we socialize, we recount, over and over, tales from Italy. How we made spaghetti, how our grandmothers made manicotti, the unification of Italy, our favorite flowers there, how people sneeze differently in Italy than here, how the mountains look different in Colorado than they do in Italy, the day we departed on the ship, where we had our first kiss. For many of us, it was Via Partenope, or the terrace at Belvederi Sorrento. We talk about our lives in Colorado, but before long, our thoughts drift to that far off place. We notice that people from other places do this, too. For us, it is Italy, but for others it is England, New York, or Germany.

What we seem to cherish above all is receiving mail from Italy. It almost seems like a miracle the mail could reach us from so far away, and that our friends and family actually touched that letter. *These words have traveled far*, I always think. We love receiving letters of any kind, from our friends, parents, aunts, cousins, neighbors, professors, teachers. These people represent our memories of our country, and memories of our former selves. The letters from there seem quaint, as if from a past life. We carry these letters with us. Women carry them in their purses. I always carry mine in my attaché case, where I keep my music; they are always with me.

The letters seem innocent; like the people writing to us have not experienced something we have. But we left that familiar place and our familiar selves. We are no longer that self, but is our current self really any better? At the Buckhorn Exchange, a tavern in the middle of Denver, this is often the topic of much conversation.

I tend to accept living in Denver and being a musician as fate. I do not question it much, but some people do. We simply boarded a ship and left. We brought ourselves with us, but ourselves are somehow transformed, like chrysalises that emerged as a slightly new species of butterflies.

The next day, the *Denver Times* reports that Father Lepore has died. He had been murdered with a gun, but also murdered his assailant. The rumors of poker were apparently false, but past business dealings were mentioned. "I believe the man was sent from Italy to kill me" were apparently Father Lepore's last words, spoken to the police, and his deathbed confession that he indeed shot the man. The last words of the article, however, are also somewhat intriguing. Could it be true?

Over and over, we read, "The Italians are so secretive, we may not ever know what really happened." There is much discussion about this in the streets and in the taverns.

Are Italians secretive, and if so, why? We all scratch our heads, yell, debate, curse our ancestors and use gestures and expressions from the old country until dawn.

CHAPTER TWELVE

"Pietro Satriano plans a very, very secret wedding."

I meet Musa Etherton late one night at the park before a performance. Miss Etherton is an attractive, refined lady. Her mother and sisters own a beauty salon in their home. Many people frequent their home, even some gentleman go there for hair treatments, I am told. Musa does hair styling for the soloist singers, or guest performers, who come from out of town to perform here.

Musa's vivacious personality acts as a catalyst. After my terrible fate with Anna, I have avoided ladies, figuring I should cut my losses and remain a single man. Some men are just not meant for marriage; the artist in me, my passions, my almost monk-like commitment to my art, preclude a good marriage, I have decided. I remember the psychic on the ship, who said I would have problems with love, and she was right. If I had not divorced, I could teach at College of the Sacred Heart and be a Jesuit, like Papa. He lived as a monk after Mama died. He loved immersing himself in music and, unfortunately, gin. But the lack of a woman in his life, I now see, led him to a musical climax, and he wrote some of his best things after Mama died. Coincidence it may be, but something in him changed then.

But as I am thinking all this, I am watching a young lady named Musa from a distance. She is styling the hair of my soloist tonight, a Miss Reed. I am in the band shell, ostensibly preparing for tonight's performance, but my attention is more drawn to Musa.

It will probably be another fiasco. I will stray and play, my angry outbursts...no, I cannot do it. Musa is much too sweet and deserving of a more steady man. My passions run deep. I put the first score on the music stand, trying hard to concentrate on performance issues. At least she is my age, I think, adjusting the height of the music stand. I arrange the chairs precisely the way I want them for the wind section, looking over at Musa, who is now curling another lady's hair and smiling and chatting with Miss Reed. I make myself focus on the performance, and not this enchanting lady. Too often, I have thought I knew which lady was right for me, and the relationships have always ended on a sour note.

A few days later, I receive a letter from Orsola, who now has eight children. In the second paragraph, the first consisting of preliminary statements about the weather and her children, I cannot believe my eyes. There, in her lovely Italian cursive writing, are the words, "there is a lady in Denver who I think you should get to know. Her name is Musa Etherton. She is a calm and gentle soul, the kind of woman you want to marry. She is originally from the fine state of Missouri, and I can assure you women from here are God-fearing, stable women."

I decide that the next time I see her, I shall make her acquaintance. The problem is the gossip. If I start dating again, it will be in the rumor mill and even the newspapers. What kind of woman would want that kind of attention, and want me, a man who receives bad press every time I walk outside?

Then, the following weekend, she saunters over to me. Smiling her sweet smile. What she says next really floors me. "Your sister said we should meet." I can't believe Orsola is a matchmaker.

I feel safe with Musa. I smile and gently touch her shoulder. "We must be discrete." She winks at me, but then stares at my hair and says, "You have been a bachelor for too long, Maestro. Let me fix your hair." I feel a bit awkward about letting a woman cut my hair. Only barbers and Mama have cut my hair before. We go behind the band shell, into a small grove of trees, and there, in the waning light of day, she cuts my hair. I always think of this as our first date. It was a calm and innocent first date.

Musa and I get married shortly after we meet. I notice that I seem to be getting more contemplative as I get older. I think about music, the spiritual beauty of music. My marriage to Musa has only served to make my music better. She is my muse, and she guides me. Although I never tell her this. I feel the sorcery of its charms all the time, and like most people, I think, feel transformed and enlivened by the charms in music. The newspapers write about my hands and arms, my gyrations, my cute two-step, my baton. But there is more to me, much more.

It is a pleasant morning, and I walk the streets with a bounce in my step. Musa tells me I walk like a musician, but what that means I am unsure, yet at the same time I am not surprised in the least. I tip my hat to the ladies I see, and have been feeling much less burdened now that I do not have to keep my drunk Papa in the band. I walk slowly past a shoe shop, *scarpes,* we call them in Italy. The sign has a touch of Italiano in its humor, in my opinion:

Don't go elsewhere to be cheated.
Walk in here.

The proprietor of the shop, Luigi, is out sweeping and whistling, as if he, too, has not a care in the world. I say to him, "Your sign is amusing."

He looks at me with surprise. "I hang this sign and I do not understand why people think it is amusing. It means we won't cheat you. Why does everyone think it funny?" He lived in New York prior to coming here, and he has an Italian lilt to his voice, plus a Brooklyn accent. He shakes his head as if a bit confused and resumes his sweeping.

This is what's funny about America. So many people, so many characters.

CHAPTER THIRTEEN

"Professor Satriano's musical library is one of the
largest in the West, approximately 3000 selections..."

Pietro

President Roosevelt is coming to Denver. There is much debate. Will it be my band performing, or will it be Rafael Cavallo, or someone else?

I am tense; this has created a moral dilemma. What if I am chosen? On top of this, Musa has given me news that she is with child and I am to be a father in six months. She has been ill, and the doctor has ordered her to stay in bed; he says the risk of a miscarriage is great. I have so much to worry about: Musa, money, my job, my reputation. And, if we have a child, a new mouth to feed.

My band and I are going to practice "The President's March," just in case. I want to be ready. I will be most proud to perform for the president. Before I came to America, this would have been a fantasy performance; to Europeans, presidents are the equivalent of royalty. But I was so naïve, thinking that America was a better place. My reluctance has to do with disdain for Mr. Roosevelt for his apparent hatred of Italians, according to a statement he publically made prior to becoming President.

Two weeks go by and I do not hear anything. One day I am sitting in my office on Sixteenth Street and I get a call from the Governor's office: I am chosen to perform for the President at a political rally at the Antler's Hotel in Colorado Springs.

The first time I met him, I was unaware of his cavalier statement about the deaths of Italian people. He came to Colorado to go hunting, and my band and I met his train at the Kansas state line. As soon as his train crossed into Colorado, it stopped and my men and I boarded the train. We welcomed him to our fine state by serenading him all the way Denver. During a break, I was asked to sit with Mr. Roosevelt. We enjoyed a good cigar together. I know nothing about hunting and very little about politics, and he knows nothing about music, so we had a nice talk.

Performing for the President is grand for my reputation, but Musa is so ill. She cannot get out of bed. She tells me to go, that I have to. Regardless of his offhand comments years ago, before he was President, about the hanging of eleven Italian people, I should go. "What an honor," she says. She does not understand why I fret about this so. At times, in some ways, I have high moral standards and in other ways, none. She prattles on about this. She does not normally talk so much; she is nervous, I can tell. She has a fever and is crying. "I will have a midwife come to stay with me tomorrow, if it will make you feel better."

Reluctantly, I perform. She is optimistic and seems better in the morning before I leave. "We'll finally have a baby here in six months, you'll see."

I feel so helpless at times like these. I really want to be a father.

Performing for the President is supposed to be an honor, an enjoyable festive occasion, but my mind is halfway always on Musa. Right after we finish several rounds of "Hail to the Chief," and "Hot Time in the Old Town Tonight" a porter from the hotel hands me a telegraph. The last time I received a telegraph was when my nephew, Peter, was born. This time I think the telegraph is about a baby, but it will be bad news rather than good. My heart sinks. I am tired from performing and traveling all day. The porter sees that I am worried. Sweat pours from my brow.

Musa Taken To Hospital STOP
Do Not Delay Come Fast STOP

The porter takes my arm, gets me through the crowd, and helps me to the train depot in Colorado Springs. The train could not have possibly moved fast enough for me. The train stops in Palmer Lake, a lovely little town that I usually enjoy stopping in, but today, the town is irritating and I hate it. It is interfering with me being with my wife.

It is such a small town, and isolated, who would ever live here? Finally, a few hours later, the train arrives at Union Station in Denver.

I practically disembark before the train completely stops. Finally, finally, I can walk at my own pace and get where I need to be at my own pace. It is good to walk, and I pretend like all I have to do is put one foot in front of the other. I turn left on Fifteenth. I focus only on walking, nothing else. I need to be somewhere and I am walking. I think of when Mama died in childbirth. What will I do if I get to the hospital and Musa has died? What if the baby has died, and not Musa? What if they both die, like when Mama died? I remind myself not to think, just walk.

I arrive at the hospital. A nurse tells me she is upstairs. I grab the wooden banister and run up, skipping two steps at a time. I find her room. She is crying. I kneel beside her bed. "I am so happy you are alive! Musa, Musa, darling, I am so sorry." I see a small cradle and look inside. The tiny baby boy is still there, his skin is cool. He apparently just died. I, too, cry, kneeling on the floor next to Musa. Nothing has ever seemed sadder to me. Musa stops crying and pats my shoulder. "Pietro, Pietro. We will be fine." I cry for a long time. A nurse comes in at one point, but Musa waves her away dismissively.

Then the doctor comes. I feel embarrassed and wipe my eyes. He says the miscarriage was hard on her, and she probably will not be able to conceive a child again. I am relieved; at least she will not have to go through this again.

It is a sad time, and I feel close to Musa, taking care of her, even cooking for her and taking care of the housework. I am extra vigilant about keeping a fire going so she will be warm, and we talk and hold hands in the evenings while we sit at the hearth. I play harp music on the gramophone to soothe us.

Musa

I am sitting by the window one snowy night, waiting for Pietro, who is attending a Denver Musicians Protective Association meeting. The windows are steaming up, the snow lying thick on the ground, like a blanket of creamy mashed potatoes. I wipe the window with my hand and press my nose against the glass to look outside. What if Pietro is stuck in the mashed potato snow somewhere? I hate to think of him suffering, but at the same time, there is something magical about him, and if he were stuck he could think of a musical or dramatic yet graceful way to pick himself up, wipe the flakes off his top coat and hat and proceed as if all in a matter of due course. It would make headlines in the paper: "Signor Satriano Temporarily Immobilized By Snowdrift. "

My vapor appears on the windows like hieroglyphic paintings that magically disappear within seconds of my last exhalation.

Rather than worry about Pietro, I write a letter to Olivia.

Dearest Olivia,

Do come for a visit. I look forward to talking, and having companionship with a lady.

My days are long without a child. Pietro seems so far away, yet he is usually in the next room. All the ladies in town are infatuated with my husband. I know this is every woman's dream, but it is hard, and I do think Pietro likes the attention of other women. I think Pietro is mysterious. I cannot wait for you to visit and tell me whether you think he is mysterious. The mystery is both a blessing and a curse. It keeps me riveted, but also insecure.

Yours truly,

Mrs. Pietro Satriano (Musa)

He comes home covered in flaky, incandescent snow, seemingly unaware that he is lit up like a gas lamp, with translucencies sparkling as they melt. "I wish I could look like this when I perform… translucent. Imagine it." He looks at himself in the mirror and smiles.

THREE MONTHS LATER

We awaken to a beautiful late spring morning. Winter's heavy snow created an array of wayward wildflowers through the valley known as Denver. The advent of spring momentarily causes this high arid desert to look like an ephemeral jungle.

The birds are singing and we are laughing because the birds' chorale is so loud; we laugh because the animals are making music, all competing with one another to be the loudest or the loveliest, depending on their personalities. The loud ones are Pietro, undoubtedly.

"We will eat on the front porch this morning," I tell him.

"Why?"

"It's a special day. I have something important to tell you."

Pietro, moving around the room, is trying to find his trousers and then he will shave. He is a man of contemplative action; he is thoughtful, yet likes movement, and does not like small talk. I am waiting to see what his response will be to my idea of breakfast on the front porch.

He smiles, the music of birds and sunshine putting him in an agreeable mood. "Yes, my love, that will be nice," he says right after putting on his spectacles at the bedside. Then looks at me squarely in the eye as if to make sure it is really me inviting him, and not some other lady. He thinks his poor eyesight is from reading musical scores by candlelight in drafty old castles when he was a musician in Italy.

While shaving, we discuss how birds really are the best coloratura artists.

We eat ham, potatoes, and eggs. Pietro, in his contemplative action, is very attuned to food. He eats actively, as if every bite counts. It can be difficult to talk to him during meals, he is focused and driven to the task at hand. I am not sure whether Pietro remembers I have something important to tell him. He enjoys his meals so. He drinks his *caffe*, as he calls it.

"Pietro, I am with child again."

Pietro stops drinking *caffe*. He looks at me as if I am an unusual musical score, and he cannot quite understand the melody.

"But the doctor said it could not happen." And then, I am so happy. I see the corner of his lips turn up; he is smiling.

"I am due in November."

It is time for me to be a father? Oh, Orsola will be so pleased. I must write to her. Are you feeling well?"

"We both seem to be fine. Will we raise our son as a musician?"

He looks like he is spitting out his *caffe*. He gets a sour look on his face, wipes his mouth, and says, "No. Whether a boy or a girl, I do not want my child raised the way I was. I would not encourage or discourage him, but I will not teach him." Pounding his fist on the table, he says it with the sternness and rightness of a military orchestra leader.

"But, Pietro, if we do not encourage him at least, he will not try. There have been generations of musicians in your family. Pray tell what he could accomplish."

"Musa, darling...what makes you think it is a boy?"

"Women's intuition. I know. I knew even when I conceived. A woman knows."

"Si, I do believe that. I shall have a son. But he will be free to be who he wants to be. A brick layer, a surgeon, even a damn journalist.

It is America, and I am an American now. Let the boy be who he wants."

He smiles, kisses me on the lips, rolls up his sleeves like he always does before he plays any instrument, and goes to the piano for his day of working. I get glimpses of him throughout the day: concentrating, trying so hard...composing, thinking, listening with such intention.

Is he dreaming about when he lived in Spain and led the band? Does he think of his Mother, the last time he saw her? Or that awful professor he had, who used to hit him if he played an unpleasant chord? Does he think of me, do I ever move him to create? On our honeymoon in Colorado Springs, we gazed at Pikes Peak and he said he loved my voice and wanted to be with me always. But since marriage, he has never asked me to sing, and seems to have forgotten that is how we met, and it was one of the things he admired about me. In our courting days, we would take long walks, and he said he was bemused by my name: Musa. Then he would whisper in my ear: "Musa, Musa, you are destined to marry an *artista*. It is meant to be..." He would bring me flowers. He made me spaghetti for dinner. We attended an opera at the Tabor Opera House, and his brother Antonio played the clarinet with the orchestra that night. It was grand to be with him; people are always very respectful to us because of his high standing in the community.

Olivia comes to visit. I love to talk with Olivia; she has the sweetest soprano voice. Even Pietro seems to awaken from his reverie and seems happy to see her. When she enters the parlor, he bows slightly, greets her warmly and resumes practicing. President Roosevelt will be coming to Denver again and Pietro will be performing for him. I invite her to stay for lunch.

We sit in the kitchen as I prepare our meal, and she asks how we are doing. I use this as a time to talk about my marriage. Olivia is one of the few I can confide in. She is an old friend, who shows up at my door at times when I need her, like on rainy Saturday mornings when Pietro is rehearsing with the band.

I make coffee and we settle for *a tete a tete*.

"Being married to him is different than I thought…"

"Well, what did you think it would be?"

"Oh, I am happy with him. He seems distant. Sometimes I think his music is more important than me. He gets so angry sometimes."

"Honey, you married an artist."

"Yes; I fell in love with his reputation, a great artist, a European artist. Oh, I am so proud, do not get me wrong. Oh, I try hard to please him, as every wife should."

"You fell in love with his persona. He has remarkable presence."

"Indeed! I look at him all day, watch him from afar as he composes and imagines."

"What else does he do?"

"He takes a walk every day. Mr. Habrl, his manager, comes to visit. Sometimes we walk together. Oh, yes, and he bought a tandem bicycle. We ride it around the lake; he tried taking it out one day on his own and crashed into the ice truck." We both giggle.

"I always thought his intensity was rather romantic."

"Indeed." I get up to check the roast. I am making a roast with squash and beans from the garden.

"He does take an interest in gardening. Oh, you should see how delighted he gets with the tomatoes. And when the corn comes up…"

"It is good that he appreciates the small things in life. Is something bothering you?"

"I worry…am I good enough for him? Does he think about Anna? I married a divorced man. A well-known man, but he has a past…"

"Some people consider it a sin to even say the word"—she lowers her voice and whispers—"divorce."

"My mother would never say the word divorce; she always spelled it: 'The people down the street are getting a d-i-v-o-r-c-e.'"

"Every man has his problems. It is the wife's duty to help him."

"Try I do, pray tell."

"He is an interesting man to you, I think. So many women do not view their husbands as interesting."

"Our situation is about to get more interesting," I say as I put the roast on the table, with some sourdough bread and beans.

"Oh, do tell!"

"I'm going to have a baby. I am already four months along. But I worry I will have another miscarriage."

"You will have a family! Think of how musically talented the child will be."

"I just wonder if there is enough room in his life for music, myself, and a child."

"Sometimes men change when they have children. He has been teaching children about music for a long time."

"Indeed, but he said he does not want to raise the child to be a musician. He thought it was too hard on his father, God rest his soul, himself, and his brothers."

Then I say something I have not particularly thought of before, "Mothers are like artists; we create children and then nurture our creations."

"Have you pointed out this observation to Pietro?"

"No, but that is a good insight. I will have to tell him that sometime when he is in a good mood. I must call Pietro to join us; the food will get cold."

Pietro comes into the room. His hair is a bit askew, but he is, as always, impeccably dressed, and very polite to Olivia. He greets her the Italian way, a kiss on each cheek.

"Signora Olivia, have you been here long?" He apparently does not remember that he greeted her an hour ago.

"An hour or so."

"Ah, I did not hear you come in. What a pleasant surprise."

We sit down at the table and eat. We are probably some of the few people who do not say grace at mealtime.

"You are looking well, Pietro; married life must be agreeing with you."

Is Olivia being slightly manipulative?

"Indeed it is," he says rather absently as he stabs the roast with a fork.

"I don't think I heard the story of why you moved here, Pietro, please tell. Why did your father come to America?"

I love to hear him talk about his previous life in Italy. He told me this story one night when we were on our honeymoon in Colorado Springs. It was a full moon, and Pikes Peak reminded me of photographs I have seen in books, of that mountain in Switzerland, the Matterhorn.

"Papa was the son of a son of a musician. It was expected of him, as it was expected that Tony and Sal and I become musicians. Papa loved music and being a musician, but by the time he left Italy, it was harder and harder to be a court musician, meaning a musician to royalty. He foresaw a time when musicians would have to earn their living other ways, and not be under the auspices of a king or queen; they are very emotional and moody, not very good at finances…much like musicians." He smiles. "Nonetheless, Papa said it could be boring. It was a lot like being a servant, at the beck and call of nobility or wealthy families, and I found it to be true as well. There were laws that said music must be performed on certain occasions, and therefore musicians had to be present to perform. There was time to compose and read, though, because the castles were in remote locations, especially the summer homes were usually in the middle of nowhere, and there was no one to talk to. The court musician system has basically ended now.

Olivia is leaning forward, looking at him like he has just told the most fascinating story.

"And tell her the other reason, Pete."

He continues, "There was a pageant. I was eleven years old. It was a major, very serious event in Italy, a religious pageant. We were marching through a city, and…I really had to use the WC. I wet my pants!" Pietro makes his funny face, his eyes widen like saucers and his mustache seems to get bigger. Olivia laughs hysterically.

"You should tell that story some time at a concert."

"No, Signora, that story remains in this house." He wags his finger at her in a playful yet firm way. "For many years I could not tell anyone that. Papa was furious. I made a spectacle of myself. I was so embarrassed. I was eleven but was expected to act like I was twenty-two. Papa believed we had to leave the country, in fact, all of Europe. The story would spread fast. He believed I was destined for greatness, but, he thought, forever more, I would be the butt of jokes in Europe. If I auditioned to be a conductor at La Scala, they would ask, 'Signor Professor Satriano…will you be able not to tinkle while conducting Pachelbel? What about Puccini, will you run off stage in haste to use the WC?' I am not so sure it was as bad as Papa thought…for many years he blamed himself for moving here. For breaking up the family."

I listen to Pietro and watch Olivia, absently running my spoon back and forth through my mashed squash, like a child. I do not realize my foolish behavior until Pietro cocks his head a bit and looks at me, and then at my plate, as if I were a daydreaming child.

"Sometimes I think I would have been happier and more respected in Italy." He looks down, returning his attention to the food.

He tells me this when we are alone sometimes, and it feels like my heart is dropping. Do I not make him happy?

Pietro has a habit of talking with his mouth full. When we dine with the governor or mayor, he never does this. But I can see he feels comfortable with Olivia, for he talks while eating bread. Little crumbs gather on his lips.

"Pietro, you are so loved here."

"Your words are kind, Signora Olivia." He winks at her and she beams with delight.

He looks at me and says, "Thank you for the meal, Musa. I must return to work."

He stands and bows slightly to both of us, his perfect posture, his beautiful brown eyes, and a trace of that lilting Italian diction... and his wonderful manners and talk when people come to visit.

We hear Pietro clearing his throat and playing notes on the piano. Olivia and I put on aprons and clear the table. She seems to be trying to pick things up quietly and gingerly, almost tiptoeing from the table to the washbasin.

"No need to do that, Olivia. He is in another world. He does not hear anything but music in his mind. He forgot that we were talking in the kitchen, or that we were even here."

Olivia and I glance into the front room, and there is Pietro, conducting an imaginary orchestra. So he can experience the full effect, he dresses for the occasion when he does this. He wears his topcoat and maestro hat. He is closing his eyes and swinging his baton, as if guiding the musicians through staccato measures.

"He is handsome and so cute."

Everything in life is a matter of perspective, I am thinking, but Olivia goes on,

"My dear, you married a musical genius. Is he a religious person?"

"He is not, and could not be, he is divorced."

"Yes, be that as it may, his musical contemplation is that of a religious man, his devotion to ritual. Do not fear, my dear, his faith is strong, his spirit is alive."

Musa

"Do not go to my study!" he yells one day, shifting around musical scores trying to find something, blaming me because he cannot find it.

"But your study is the whole house!"

"You may walk across the study to get to other rooms in the house, of course, but please do not linger unless I am present."

"Are you hiding something from me?"

"No, I am just accustomed to having music just so. I have more than three thousand pieces of music; I have one of the largest music collections in the Western United States."

"I believe this is true, as anyone who walks into our home could clearly see." Keeping house with two thousand music scores is impossible. He keeps about a thousand scores at his office.

"Perhaps you can get a bigger office."

"Yes; I can see your point," he says, looking around the stacks and stacks of music, and for the first time ever, even *he* seems bewildered by it all. "It would be an extra expense, but…I will look into it. We have more money now. Mr. Habrl has an office on Sixteenth Street, and he may have some space." He sighs, shakes his head as if he has one more problem in life, and returns to his music.

I am surprised; usually he does not acquiesce to what I want. I kiss him on the cheek, and he smiles his boyish smile.

Then he sits down at the piano bench, one of the few places to sit that is not stacked with sheet music.

"I have been thinking about what to name our son."

"Oh…what do you think?" I am pleased he is thinking of this. He really can be sweet and sentimental, and I thought we were going to have a big fight about music all over the house, but that does not seem important now. Pietro seems to be a little more sensitive to my feelings lately. The ladies at the beauty parlor tell me sometimes men change when they are going to become fathers…

"We live in America, and people do not have to name their sons after the paternal grandfather first, then the second son after the maternal grandfather, and the third son after the father…If you went to Naples and called out the name Pietro at the market, or a great music hall, do you know how many men would answer? There would be a stampede!"

We both giggle.

Then he is quiet. He looks down and says solemnly, "I think we should name our son...Carroll." He says the name with great cadence.

"A musical name. Yes, I like it. Carroll. Our son shall be Carroll. I cannot think of a better name for our son."

Then he starts playing a nice jaunty tune he and his brothers have been working on, "Three For Tea," a song about young lovers imagining their future together. Becoming a father seems to be lifting his spirits some, and mine, too.

CHAPTER FOURTEEN

"That Great Satriano,

with his head, legs, body and arms."

Pietro

I ride my horse to Garden of the Titans. Many musicians come to be alone here, to experience this amazing composition of red rock formations whose confluence somehow conspires to bring forth all the gods and goddesses and make music sound beautiful. Musicians informally call this area Musician Rocks, but others want to change the name to Red Rocks, to simply call it what it is.

What I did not tell Musa is that I am meeting a businessman here today, a Mr. York, a wealthy man in Denver. I want him to see this place.

I wait and wait, and finally see him in the distance. His horse is slowly creeping along the rocky ridge, kicking up dust. Mr. York is slouched down. He looks a bit irritated that I have caused him to come all this way. He has a scowl on his face, and I am bracing myself, thinking this meeting was not a good idea. He could be sitting in a tavern right now, sipping sherry or having a luncheon at a men's club. Instead, I have dragged him out to the edges of civilization.

He calls to me, "Pietro, dagnabbit, this is Injun country! What are you doing here?" The dust is causing him to cough into a red bandana.

"But Mr. York, look at these cliffs. Look! Off to the left, it looks like something from outer space. And notice our echo..."

"Yes, yes..." he says absently. "Why did you want me to see this place?" He dismounts his horse.

My heart sags. If he cannot see why I would bring him here... "I thought it would be obvious to you. There is money to be made here."

"How? Why? Letting the savages sell jewelry and pottery?"

"No, Signor York. Look up. It is set like a stage. Nature made it a theatre. The Indians have been here for centuries, playing music and having ceremonies." I help Mr. York stand; he is stiff from the long ride up here. I turn all directions, north, south, east and west, so that he will mimic me. He looks at the cliffs, first low and then high. I sense he is starting to see things my way.

"Imagine...this is the stage. The beauty will attract people from far away. Where else are concerts given among such beauty?" I can see it in his eyes, he is starting to dream.

But I am wrong. He says in an irritating voice, "I could be having a scotch and soda right now. Instead, you bring me out to this dust," he coughs.

It is dusty here, I agree. And windy. A big gust of wind blows through from the west, and we both grab our hats. But I am intent on keeping him focused on one thing: let's get this place to be a musical place, where people will come for generations to experience music. I start again, competing with the wind:

"...Imagine, the entrance right there. People buying tickets to see this magnificent place. The best entertainers will want to perform here."

He puts his head down and kicks at the ground with his boots. "But it is so far away. It took a whole day to get here by horse."

"You have power. Get the streetcar or the trains to come. Electric cars will be here soon. Start stagecoach runs. Ladies love it when their husbands hire a carriage for the evening and bring them to the park to see my shows. There is a lodge here too. Build another lodge."

"I see some potential here, maybe, but not now. Pie in the sky dreaming, if you ask me. All you Italians are dreamers."

I ignore his mildly snide comment. "I can get the entertainers to come, leave that to me."

The sun passes behind huge clouds, causing the rocks to look ominous. These summer afternoon clouds and thunderstorms are a unique part of being a Coloradan. They are as reliable as the sun setting in the west and rising in the east.

"What about the weather? I would need to make a better road, at least. And seats, and a concession stand."

"Maybe not. Let's have one concert. We will advertise in the newspaper that it is a concert in the mountains, a way to escape city life. Once they know about Garden of the Titans, they will come."

The sky is growing dark. Rain is sure to fall momentarily. There is drama in the aroma of rain; aroma appears on stage first, meant to tease and entice, before the main event. Just then, lightning strikes and nearly hits the large rock that looks like a ship. We both stand in awe.

"That was amazing. The crackle of the lightning. The brightening of the sky, and then gentle rain. What a performance."

"See what I mean, about the weather..." Mr. York grumbles.

"But there are thunderstorms in Denver every afternoon, too..." I try to make light of the rain.

"Yes; but there are places to take shelter. I can tell by the look in your eye you want it to happen, boy. Why?"

"I came to America..." I start to get choked up. There is no place to go for relief from the rain. We are standing in the mud, holding umbrellas. I have to talk louder, over the rain and now distant thunder. The whole thing seems surreal, and I am feeling silly about my desire to turn this into a performance theatre. He may be right, I fear. Papa always told me I had fanciful ideas.

The rain persists, but so do I. I try again: "I came to America to be a great musician…Father said I am a leader in the music world. But here I am in Denver. What can I do? I am an Italian cowboy musician. This is not what I wanted. I want to make something unique. Garden of the Titans will be a lasting tradition. "

Mr. York takes out his pipe. Mud is gathering all around us, and that first hint of sunshine after a brief, intense storm. We are both wet, the brims of our hats dripping rain, looking like two foolish men who lost their horses and are down on their luck.

"I am staying at the lodge tonight. I will think on the matter. It is intriguing. You know, it is old men like me who make money off of young people's fancies."

With that, he climbs on his horse, gives me a look as if he still thinks I am a lunatic, and starts to ride off.

I know in my heart I've convinced him. I know this will be a gathering place for music and no longer only known to musicians and Indians, whose families have come here for generations, to make music.

My attention is drawn to a man riding a horse toward us at a full gallop. "Signor Satriano? You need to return to Denver. Your wife is in the hospital."

I do not remember many details, except that a mining train takes me back to Denver. I am never there when she needs me. Once I arrive in Denver, I nervously ride the streetcar to the hospital. Why does it move so slowly, and how come I never noticed its slowness before? Then I alight the streetcar and try to calm myself. I tell myself all the things I told myself the last time: I am merely going for a walk, as if I have an appointment at the hospital and simply need to get there quickly. I walk fast, trying not to think. She is nine months along. The baby is full term. Surely, this time, she will be fine. But Mama was nine months pregnant, too, and…

I stop thinking and just walk. The ladies must have thought me to be quite rude, for I did not greet anyone or tip my hat. Tomorrow, it will be in the gossip column in one of the papers that I really should mind my manners. Again.

When I walk into her room, I am relieved. She is lying in the hospital bed smiling, holding a baby with curly blond hair. Carroll Pietro Satriano. I am so relieved and the whole world temporarily seems musical, like a fantasia of music everywhere. I am one proud Papa.

And, as every musician dreams, now I have my muse and my carroll.

Once Musa and Carroll are home from the hospital, I tell Musa about my talk with Mr. York.

She is always so kind and encouraging. Mama would have liked her. "Pietro, that is just what you need!"

"Yes, a large concert up on the rocks. Will they come, though? That is what concerns Mr. York."

"The trolley may go there someday, Denver is growing."

Indeed, the census a few years ago said Denver's population grew by more than thirty thousand people between 1890 and 1900.

"I want you to come with me. You have got to hear the sound there. And there is an Indian I see sometimes. He plays a wooden flute, like none I have ever heard. I call him Blackfoot. One foot is blacker than the other; I think it may be a scar, so I call him Blackfoot. He listens and appreciates music, I can tell."

"You should not be among savages! Pray tell what could happen."

"Musa, do not worry, I will be fine. I think the Indians are peaceful people. Most of them harm only when they are being attacked. The Garden makes people, men or beast, feel invigorated, and reminds us of the beauty of life."

"To have a name like Garden of the Titans, it must be *benissimo*."

"It might also smooth things over with the public, and my manager. Since my angry outburst a few years ago with those visiting cornet soloists…" It is the first time I have mentioned it since that performance fiasco that everyone thought was so terrible.

"Frankly, Pietro, I don't know if there is anything you can do to change that, but it is good to try."

"A man with a vision, I am." I wiggle my spectacles for show. I put on my top hat and head out for some gin.

Musa

Pietro has been on edge lately; he has to write a piece for a performance with an orchestra. He has been festering about it, on edge, ruminating. Even more than usual. He feels like he cannot quite make it grand enough. That is why he was so angry with me for moving some of his musical scores earlier; he is just nervous, and trying to write a grand opus. He loves to compose. In addition, he is disappointed because Mr. York was not interested in turning Garden of the Titans into a performance venue. I lie in bed, unable to sleep.

Maybe I could help him. Do I dare? Should I? I am feeling bold.

I cannot resist. He is sleeping beside me. He tells me he dreams only of cornets, sonatas and band performances, but I suspect he dreams about more than he lets on. I carefully pull back the covers, put on my house slippers, and tiptoe to the piano. It is very early in the morning, 4 o'clock; apparently it is my witching hour. I quietly sit at the piano bench, where I have never sat before, and look at the aria he is working on. The soprano solo seems too high to me. I take it down about a third and change a few notes in the measure preceding it. I see more I could rearrange, but oh, he will be so angry with me.

I tiptoe back to bed, and he is sleeping, in an unknown world only his mind occupies. He could not possibly get any angrier with me than he already is. I feel like a mischievous child, wanting to make him even angrier at me. Why, I am unsure. He does not always know my strengths or appreciate my virtues. I, too, know about music, and he could learn something from me.

CHAPTER FIFTEEN

"Music lovers of the city turned out en masse…"

Pietro May 31, 1906

My dream for a concert at Garden of the Titans will become a reality this afternoon. Shortly after Mr. York told me I was *pazzo*, a Mr. John Brisben Walker bought the property to be a performing arts arena, like so many musicians have thought it should be for a long time. Mr. Walker and most musicians envision the same dream. And, my band and I shall be the first to perform there.

When I first received word that Mr. Walker bought the property, I was thrilled. However, I feel guilty: the Indians love and revere Garden of the Titans; it is sacred to them, and we are going to take it away, and it will never be the same. It is one more slice of nature slipping away from them.

Musa and I, and Mr. Walker and his wife, spend the night at the Cliff House, a beautiful lodge near Garden of the Titans. We celebrate. Mr. Walker and I have hope and high expectations that the concert will be the beginning of something extraordinary. Musa seems to be enjoying herself, although at times she looks distant and worried. We had to leave Carroll in Denver with her sisters; he is still a baby.

I tell Mr. Walker what Mr. York later told me. After our first meeting up here, he came up to Garden of the Titans a second time, and watched me from a distant cliff. The scene was memorable, seeing an obviously Italian man swaying in reverie to ethereal-sounding flute music, then closing his eyes to his own horn. He noted my horn playing sounded different when playing with an Indian, as if the Italian had become a savage person.

Mr. York decided not to interfere with our little performance. He rode to the Titans to talk to me about a new idea he had for a performance, but quickly changed his mind when he saw me with "a savage."

I remember that day, although I did not know Mr. York was watching. I was playing cornet with Blackfoot. We worked out an interesting melody that harmonized flute with cornet. I play softly because the sound reverberates so swiftly, like a slingshot bouncing off the cliffs. Blackfoot's flute was so soft that it echoed through the timeless cliffs and sounded so peaceful.

There are many people staying at the lodge for the concert. I love to meet the public. They are always respectful to me. I am worried about the weather because afternoon thunderstorms are always a threat. Mr. Walker insisted the concert be in the afternoon, as many people are coming by horseback or carriages from Denver. A few are driving automobiles, they say, although I cannot imagine because these old dirt trails are footpaths carved by Indians and various animals. Sometimes the trails end abruptly, as if everyone who has ever ridden a horse on them suddenly remembered something they forgot to do. There is also a special train running from Denver to Morrison for this special event. Many people consider the cost for a round trip ticket to be absurd. *Twenty-five cents!*

We will give them time to get here. I wish Papa could be here. Tony and Sal are coming for the performance and will take a photograph of me performing and will send it to professors and conductors we know in Italy. They said there is nothing like Garden of the Titans in Italy. I countered there is nothing like this in the world.

Before leaving home, I went to the attic. I looked through some old boxes and found the jar of goose fat and the ring. I had not looked at these things in ten years, at least. The goose fat jar made me smile. The ring, I never understood my lack of attachment. It made me angry. But now, I look at it and feel some warmth toward it. It used to be on Professor Romano's hand. Why have I not worn it all these years? I place it on my finger. He told me it would protect me, and I could use all the help I can get right now because of this experiment, up at the place where the rocks appear to be a very deep pink, or a light reddish color, and miraculously form a natural amphitheater.

Before the performance, my alone time, I look at the ring. A gold band, the hint of a dark outline, and no inscription. When I came to America, I was at the gateway of my art, but thought I knew everything. Music has a way of revealing itself over time; similar to this ring I am finally wearing, its secrets revealing itself to me all these years later.

Enough of this existential chatter. I shine my shoes to the point that they are virtually translucent; they look like black olives in Italy, shiny and moist with dew right before harvest. I have my pocket watch, my baton, jar, and I am ready.

At three o'clock, I tell my musicians it is time to perform. Often, the storms start right at three, as if the angels have pocket watches and cry at the same time every day. I help the musicians get warmed up. This is my moment, I just know. People are starting to come. They are looking around, straining their necks, to see this place. They look to north, east, south and west just like Mr. York and I did. They find the place amusing, but once the music starts, they will be mesmerized. It will be the same effect as when I performed for King Alphonso of Spain, when I was only seventeen. No one was expecting much, and then there is this young boy on stage...

I give my musicians a talk. They do not share my enthusiasm for this place; they do not have the vision. No one is to be off time tonight, I tell them, using my baton as an extended index finger. Play it well and we will get to perform here again. I give them my stern look that I learned from the old masters: No nonsense tonight. Mr. Walker walks onto the wooden platform that serves as our stage and welcomes the audience and introduces us. He gazed toward the sky. "We trust the rain will cooperate for this first official concert here at Garden of the Titans." It was as if he were giving the heavens an admonition.

Just then, coming up the ledge of the dirt path along the cliffs, I squint a bit. Tony and Sal appear to be walking with an elderly gentleman. It cannot be. No, no.

My heart races. Is this a dream, another musical apparition? Maybe I am just excited. But no, it is not that. It is…him! Professor Romano, all the way from Italy. I cannot believe he is still living and made the trip. Professor Romano! I leap off the platform and run toward him like a little child. He is still a bit frail, but seems more robust than he did in Italy. Sal, Tony, and Musa are all smiling at me; they arranged this surprise and seem really happy, too. Father Romano is here, at the Garden of the Titans. It is amazing, and I am so grateful to my brothers…

His manner and voice are the same, that of Old World Italy, which I have not heard in a long time. "I have traveled far to hear you, Pietro Antonio. I told you I would come to America when you are famous" he said in Italian.

He sits on the ground and rests after the long journey from Denver. My brothers leave to find a chair. I embrace him and his scent conjures up so many memories; he still smells like flowers and vino and the musty, soothing smell of old Italy. I thought he was very old when I was young in Italy, but he seems younger now. During our greetings, he said he overcame tuberculosis, and feels better than he did then. When one is young I guess everyone seems old. He hands me an old baton. "It was your Papa's and your

Grand Papa's. It has "Satriano" imprinted on the side, and someone sent it to Milan, thinking it was yours.

"I cannot believe it! Papa would be so pleased. He spoke about his baton all the time and missed it so." I shall use it during the performance; it is an omen.

The clouds were a godsend, because I did not have to squint to see the music, and I could look at the public without a scowl on my face. Candles and lamps were lit on stage, which gave the concert a sacred feel, as well it should. I begin the first strains of the "Holy City." There is the quintessential feeling of magical anticipation.

The audience is hushed. They never heard anything like it. "A perfect sounding phonograph turned up very high," they said later. The natural cliffs are soundboards that protrude from the earth. There are some sprinkles, as the Americans call it, but no outbursts. The angels colluded with us in late May, which is most unusual; mud season in Colorado, they call it. I worry that people will leave during the sprinkles, but no, they sit, mesmerized. One knows when the crowd is mesmerized. Musicians know when it is good and when it is not good; we know. I do not need to speak to them or hear them to know. A musician knows. We enchant them.

For the first time, I am happy my father brought me here, to the middle of nowhere, for me to make a name for myself and be recognized as a musician. I just feel like it is the start of something grand; a juxtaposition of music and nature for generations to come. I smile. The next day, the *Denver Times* mentions the smile on my face. "His coattails flew as he leaped from one side of the makeshift wooden stage to the next. Signor Satriano was in fine form last night. He has never been observed smiling during a concert, but yesterday, smile he did."

Musa

Pietro is often like a man in a dream state. He composes, then he stares off into space. He lights a cigar, puffs on it for a while, then puts it out as if he ingested what he needed, then goes back to dreaming. He will play a few notes on the piano, sometimes play a long time, sometimes only a few chords, and then seem to be in a dream state again. The whole house is a mess of scores. The living room, the hallway, the bedrooms. The music gets musty smelling. The only room where there is not music is in my domain, the kitchen. I even find scores taped to the wall in the bathroom, over the bathtub. He thinks about music in the tub. He sings in there. He is a bit awkward about his singing, and ironically cannot carry a tune. I ask him why, and he does not know. He tried to learn. Children at the Royal Academy of Music teased him about it when a cornet teacher would ask him to hum a tune before he played it.

The sheet music is his. If I touch it, or try to organize it, he goes into a rage. He screams, "Do not touch it! It is mine! Damn it to hell, you touched it!" or "what have you done? You have ruined my work." I will say I was straightening up, or just trying to help, and he looks at me, lifts his nose and snarls, as if I am the hired help.

It is the same kind of rage that the newspaper reports when he gets mad at a performer. His mysteriousness is what attracted me to him originally, but now it seems to be the problem. I think of him as a musician, not as a husband. I try to talk to my friends about this, Olivia, Mildred, and Helen, but…there are just some things women do not talk about. Mildred's husband is a milkman and Helen's husband owns an apothecary. I do not think they understand him. It is probably his musical mind, they say. He is an artist and so popular. Mildred's wife complains how boring her husband is, talking about delivering milk and eggs, and which families owe him money. She is convinced that her neighbor, Mrs. Smith, is having an affair with her husband. She laughs and says, "I think she butters him up and eggs him on."

I have quite the opposite problem; in some ways, it sounds very pleasant to be married to a boring man. Pietro is anything but boring. Helen says her husband enjoys reading about all the new mixtures and elixirs that are available these days, and how medicine is advancing. They are in awe of me, being married to such a talented, well-known man. I keep things to myself, things about him. Those rages he goes into, that at times cause him to be a victim, although he cannot see this.

He was not like this when we first met, always impeccably dressed, so courteous and amusing, and a good listener. When I comment on this, during one of our nightly strolls around the park, he comments, "All musicians are good listeners." He tried to be appealing, tried to be sophisticated, fashionable, and coy all at the same time, and succeeded. But even through this, there was a part of him that was not there; his mind was adrift, as if separate from him. I think it is his musical mind. With his arms and musical imagination, it seems like he could reach the mountains, reach all the way to Mt. Evans, like he could orchestrate moving mountains with a wave of his baton, if he willed.

Tonight when he returns home late from a performance, he seems in a companionable mood. We have the windows open and it is a beautiful summer night, the cicadas making their own August symphony. He is his old self, gentle and relaxed, probably due to a good show that night. We talk amicably about the summer evening, our new front porch, and about the picture show we are going to see tomorrow. He likes Rudolph Valentino and I like Charlie Chaplin, who reminds me of Pietro. We debate for a while about who is the better actor, but then, I venture into what I thought was a good topic of conversation:

"I read that new score you have been working on so intensely."

"You should not read my private papers."

"But I am your wife, and it is a beautiful song."

"You do not know your place in my life."

"I am supposed to support and encourage you. How am I to do so if you do not share with me? Are you a tortured soul?"

Pietro sits up in straighter. He looks genuinely surprised by my candor, not angry.

There is a long pause. He looks toward the sky, as if the answer to my question were there, hovering in the clouds. "I suppose I am, very much so. It is the curse of being a man of music."

He takes off his spectacles, rubs the bridge of his nose and says, "At least you do not break my spectacles the way Anna did."

He kisses me and goes to sleep.

Pietro

I have been asked to dine with the Governor and Mayor Speer, a very industrious fellow who supports the arts. We have been invited to a formal dinner, and I will be conducting the orchestra during an after-dinner concert. It will allow me to conduct and return to one of the instruments I love to play, the violin.

Musa is all excited, and she and her sisters are here today to help make a special dress. They are gathered around in the parlor, all laughing and happy. They are discussing whether the dress should be "off the shoulder," which I guess is the new modern style. The dress must be silk, they say, with a corset and a lace train. They see me walk into the room and their attention turns to me.

"What will Pietro wear?" They look and sound a bit hopeless, as if I am the frog taking the princess to the dance.

It is decided after much frivolous discussion that I shall don a black coat with tails, a wing tip collar and a white waistcoat with white gloves. Oh, and black stripes of satin along the outside seam of my trousers, I believe that is what they said. It sounds fancy to me, and I rather like to wear formal dress on festive occasions.

Two weeks later, Musa and I are dressed in our new clothes, and we take an electric automobile to the governor's home. It is a nice evening, and some people are gathered in the front yard, some playing croquet, the men smoking cigars, the women fanning themselves. My band members have been asked to enter later, through the back door.

The evening is grand, and Musa and I waltz. Musa later dances with the governor, and I dance with the governor's wife. The strings sound wonderful; the acoustics in the mansion are good.

During our meal, for which about twenty people are present, we discuss Molly Brown and President Roosevelt. We drink champagne out of fine crystal glasses that make a wonderful clinking sound. The ladies all look so pleasant and refined, and everyone appears to be aglow because of the vino and modern gas lamps. The cigars are excellent, supposedly brought directly to the governor's mansion from Cuba.

As always seems to happen at these gatherings, the topic turns toward Italian Americans and music. It is my time to educate people. People think the first opera was performed in New York, but actually it was in New Orleans in 1836.

One woman wearing a large hat with feathers exclaims, "But they hang Italians there!" And she is correct; where we are most revered we are also most despised.

"But why was it in New Orleans, not New York?" asks a bespectacled genteel-appearing man.

"The ships went a southerly route, because of trade and better weather, before regular routes to New York were established. We brought opera with us. The common Italian music has become popular music for American bands as well. The Italian bands contributed to the unique style of music that is coming out of New Orleans."

There is much chatter about this, and people seem intrigued that a lot of American music has an Italian influence.

Everyone is quiet for a moment and I say, "The largest lynching on American soil was in 1891." I blurt this out on impulse, wanting these people who are primarily of white, Protestant descent to know this. It is on my mind, festering all the time. Musa kicks me under the table. People look at me, suddenly silent. I continue, not surprised by their hushed response. "A police chief was murdered. Italians were accused of the murder and had their day in court and were found not guilty, or a mistrial was declared for a few. A group of people were upset about the verdict and dragged the defendants outside, along with two other Italian people who happened to be in court, and hanged them."

"Oh, horrible, horrible!"

"What kind of people would do such a thing?"

"Monstrous, preposterous!"

"Unconscionable," barely audible.

Several people speak out, astonished, but are they just the responses they think are the correct ones, or do they really believe what they are saying?

"I have been out walking the streets of our fine city and had nefarious-looking people say to me, 'Who killa de chief?' which I think is quite cruel and taunting." My spine tingles, and my head feels like someone has just smashed it with large cymbals. To wrap up my little lesson in educating white, wealthy, Protestant people, I say, "President Roosevelt, before he became President, said the lynchings 'were a rather good thing.'"

I throw my napkin on the chair and leave, before I become angry and have one of my infamous tirades. I am sure they would have liked to see it; they hear about my tirades, but does it ever occur to them that Italians have plenty to be angry about?

When it is close to the time my band and I are to perform, I go to use the restroom. There is someone using the facilities, so I wait outside the door and watch the scenes of merriment and business dealings. I enjoy the new style of women wearing dresses that are rounder and more open at the neck, which seems to be more flattering for the ladies and more intriguing for the gentlemen. This daydreaming is interrupted by a rather loud man who looks at me and says, "Hey, Black Boy, bring me a drink."

I turn around and look at the man because I am unsure as to whom he is speaking, but he is, indeed, speaking to me. He is wearing a topcoat and tuxedo, but had not been part of the governor's table. I have not seen him before but quickly reason that he may be a visiting politician or businessperson from a different city.

"I am not a servant here, sir, I am sure there is a servant nearby who can be of help."

"If you are not a servant, then why are you standing here? Shouldn't you be in the kitchen, fixing food?"

"I am a musician. My name is Pietro Satriano."

"You look like you don't belong here. An Italian, eh? Almost worse than niggers, if you ask me."

"Sir, I would be happy to bring you a drink. I would hate for your expectations of me to be ruined. The sherry is quite good. May I bring you a glass?" He does not respond, but I go to the bar myself and pour him a tall glass of sherry.

Walking toward him with the glass, I try to control myself. I try to talk myself out of it. *Pietro, do not do it, do not do it.* But it is just too enticing not to. He is seated in a red velvet chair, and I stand as close to him as I can. I smile, look down at him, and I see small hairs sticking out of his nostrils and ears. "Here is your drink, sir," and then I intentionally pour it directly onto his white winged shirt, just like mine. I chose the sherry because it stains so wonderfully.

He stands up. All I can do is stare at the stain I made. He is ranting and cursing. All the attention is on him. "You damned nigger, Italian...whatever you are..." He is flustered and flushed, and now embarrassed by his own ranting. The serving staff rushes over to him, trying to blot out the stain on his shirt. The governor's assistants ask him to please mind his language. He looks like a fool, trying to blame me for spilling a drink on him.

He leaves immediately. I like to think that if he had not voluntarily left, he would have been escorted out, but I am unsure of this.

The women murmur about immoral language, and poor, poor Pietro. But the Italians are faring well in Denver, are they not? There is much discussion, but I need to get ready for the performance.

The evening is still very pleasant, because I feel energized for speaking out against inhumanity and for performing beautiful music. It is perhaps a bit marred by that sinister man, but still wonderful.

On the way home, Musa is a little upset with me, knowing somehow that spilling the sherry was intentional on my part. I ask how she knew, but she does not say. Her intuition, she would have said. Or, *I know you better than you know yourself.*

"Your family is of British ancestry, and you do not know what it is like to be picked upon because of one's family or place of origin. The Negros, the Indians, the Italians, the Jews. Why? Why are they, or we, any better or worse than anyone?" I say.

"Did you not confirm in that man's mind that Italians are lower than snakes' bellies by your actions?"

"He will never be of a different opinion, so it does not matter. It would not matter what I did or did not do. If he had stayed to hear the band, he still would have been of the impression that I know about music, and am quite good, but I am still a lowly Italian, or nigger; I am not sure what he believes I am."

"What were you hoping to accomplish?"

"Maybe, just maybe, I made him think."

The rest of the automobile ride home is quiet, and we hold hands, the uniqueness of the evening drawing us closer.

CHAPTER SIXTEEN

"The eccentricities of genius, the peculiarities of celebrities
and the stamp of originality have found a forceful example
in the Denver band leader."

Pietro

That damn newspaper reporter telephoned again today. Wants
to do another story about me. I like all the publicity, and am
happy to be popular here in Denver, doing what I love, what a
musician does. I love the attention, the respect from the mayor,
governor, the senators, all the business owners, musicians, the ladies
and entertainers from far away. The reporters write about my
style, the music I perform, who plays for me in my band. There is
a whole side to me they do not know, and it will not be in the
paper. I would like it if sometime a reporter asked me deeper
questions about my philosophy of music. Why does he never ask
what I do in my spare time? Whether I miss Italy? Here is what I
would tell the damn reporters:

Music makes me feel intoxicated. I cannot imagine any other
occupation, a horse thief, a restaurant owner, a doctor or a farmer.
For me, life happens through music, and no one is there except
music. It is the only reality…

I am imagining the quizzical look on the reporter's face as he
sits in my parlor, smoking a pipe. He would say, "Signor Satriano,
are you sure you want that statement to go to press?" Perhaps not,
maybe he would run out the door and put it on the front page.

A major task, trying to write music, earn a living as an entertainer, be an American, and a husband. I have talked about this with Bellstedt, Cavallo, Sousa, and my brothers. Musa is right, I am a tormented man. I can never complete all of my tasks.

I don my maestro clothes, pick up my large baton, and strive, entice, border on fulfilling but only implying, suggesting and then releasing. It brings forth momentary disarray, then intensification, and then there is calm. Much like the sexual relationship between man and woman. My mind is of the Italians; we would talk about this openly. Americans keep these thoughts to themselves, and seem to be more practical and prudish about their emotions and experiences.

Papa told me about the flecks of dust that appeared in his class one day, when he became philosophical. I believe it may be true; he may have called forth the angels.

I think of my soloist at performances, singing. I believe her voice is beautiful, but what would I know? I have an unusual voice and cannot sing well. When she sang at the park the other night I saw a thin band of light coming out of her mouth. A moonlight apparition, perhaps, but nonetheless, I saw something as she sang a sweet melody. Her voice was clear and she looked beautiful, almost heavenly. Did other people see the light coming out while she sang? How could I ask? What would Mr. Habrl, or Musa, or anyone in the band say? A band of air? Pietro, are you feeling unwell? Perhaps my father and I are prone to musical apparitions, or just dreamy. Papa said it takes a certain kind of person to see these things, and see them I do.

I will be conducting the Denver Municipal Band again this summer starting on May 30, and will play ragtime, but there will be grand and comic opera nights often as well.

The paper says I have been mesmerizing the crowds of people who throng to see me. I was quoted as saying we would play the hot old airs, because that is what some people want to hear. But even people who love classical music occasionally want to hear something else. Classical music requires concentration and one must grasp what the composer is attempting to convey.

I do not believe there is a town in the United States that has more people who enjoy such a broad range of music. It will be fun and challenging for my band. We will give the people what they want. I am still a classical musician, but ragtime embraces the new, different way of life in America, and it especially speaks to younger people and people from different cultures.

From my office on Sixteenth Street, I watch a lady undress in front of a window. In the late afternoon around 4:00 p.m., I see her walk into the building across the street. She is dressed like an attractive, average young lady. But then, day after day, I see her slowly undress without closing the curtains. She always takes off her stockings slowly, and looks confidently out the window to see whether anyone is observing her.

I have come to greatly look forward to these afternoons of watching a woman who feels comfortable enough with her body to do this. I saw her on the streets numerous times before I noticed her ritual. She is always well dressed and mannerly. Most days, after a while, I see men enter and then the curtain closes. After a while, the man leaves, looking a bit disheveled, lighting a cigar, his topcoat draped over his arm and his hair a bit messy.

I buy opera glasses so I can see her better. The clerk at the store is bemused, "Signor Satriano, you are always on stage, why would you need these?" I forget now what I told her: I am getting them for my wife, or I do occasionally see other shows, or I have taken up the genteel sport of bird watching.

This woman is not a professional performer, but she puts on a good show, nonetheless.

I was somewhat obsessed with her, I admit. But gradually I am becoming disinterested in watching her through my opera glasses.

The poor lady, who undresses in front of open windows, and only closes the curtains for superficial intimacy.

One day, I hear the tires of a motorcar screeching and a lady screaming. I look out the window and there is the lady, lying on the sidewalk, her face covered with blood, her eye swollen, and she is crying. I run across the street, and at first she thinks I, too, am going to harm her, and she tries to get away.

"I want to help, I want to help you…" I take her into my office and give her some ice for the wounds on her face.

She is a streetwalker, a lady of the evening, a prostitute. Her body is enticing, but the men who call on her are troublesome.

I learn that her name is Violet, and ask why this is her chosen occupation. She says she is unable to find a job, and grew up on a farm in Kansas. She is soft-spoken and seems so vulnerable. I immediately decide to give her a job as my secretary, to get her off the streets. I really do not need a secretary, but want to help her. She is very hesitant at first, and worries the men she works for will come and beat her up for refusing to do that kind of work anymore. I feel like I need to protect her, and the lust I once felt for her is replaced by thinking of my office almost as a social service agency, and not that of a prominent musician's office. A few times her streetwalker friends come by, and we talk to them about finding jobs and where to get help.

My heart goes out to streetwalkers; it brings back memories from when I was a student at conservatories in Europe. Many boys, a few girls, no parents, and lots of housemothers and fathers to look after us, plus a few professors. Most of the people were good, but there were a few caretakers and professors who took advantage of un-chaperoned children. Their power over us was not only musical. Some of the adults used the boys for their own purposes. It was a silent and unspoken ritual among some of the faculty, and it likely ruined some of the boys who had amazing potential. We were at their mercy, and the sadists took advantage of some of the children with beatings and rapes and other atrocities. It happened to me only once. I told Professor Romano and the man was terminated from employment. From that day on, I slept in an adjoining room to Professor Romano's study, and was always safe there.

Many of the boys ran away, but sometimes they were caught and brought back. Some of them never were caught, and I would see them sitting in the streets near the conservatories in Milan and Naples, caught in the same trap of needing money and being taken advantage of. And, I could have easily been one of those boys myself.

I have seen boys going into that same building where Violet used to go. My heart goes out to those boys, too, as they are too young to be seeing a prostitute or working as prostitutes.

This lady Violet is likely a victim of her past circumstances, and is trying to control her life as best she can.

Working for me, within the confines of a safe and respectable environment, she starts to brighten as time goes on. Her true personality comes out, and she becomes less scared and more confident. She is proud of her job as my secretary, and exceptionally efficient with filing and scheduling performances and meetings. After a while, she becomes warm and outgoing with me.

I absolutely do not intend for it to happen, but my caring for her soon develops into romance, and memories of watching her through my opera glasses replace my perception that she is an injured victim, and then those thoughts are replaced with the image of being her lover.

CHAPTER SEVENTEEN

"He's the cutest thing that ever happened
when he does the cakewalk to his own music."

Musa and Pietro

Once the sun begins to rise, I dress for the day, and he awakens slowly. Usually he is up by now. I open the front door, and on the stoop is the *Denver Times*. I glance through the paper and find a headline that reads "Green Eyed Monster Strikes City Park Band."

Oh my, what has Pietro done now? As the wife of a public figure, I know to ask my husband about news in the paper first, to hear his side of the story, and get the rest of the story as it may fall.

Then I remember the middle of the night, when he came home; something was amiss. Usually, after concerts, Pietro is tired and comes home early and collapses into bed. Last night, he came in late, long past the hour of midnight. The sound of his footsteps, usually in perfect syncopation as if he were walking with a metronome, were off. I knew immediately: he is drunk. That irregular gait, the late hour. It sounded like he collapsed on the piano, the discordant sound of random keys being struck indiscriminately, as if by an angry child. Pietro would never do that. *At the tavern, vino again.*

At the kitchen table, Musa hands me the paper. Rather than devour it, page-by-page, like I normally would, I put it down hastily, absently on my toast and coffee. I drink my coffee, staring out the window.

"We must talk about this, Pietro."

There is no movement, no sound.

"Pietro, you must apologize to the public."

"I cannot."

"Pietro, you let your emotions get the best of you. You made a mistake."

He stands, stabbing his chest repeatedly with his index finger, staccato with his words: "I am the best cornetist in this country, and one of the best in the world."

"You must share the stage. They were honoring you by being there. If you were a lesser musician or bandmaster, they would not have bothered to come on the train all the way to Denver."

Eyes glistening, he says, "Musa, I cannot. I am respected. I cannot admit a mistake. It will ruin my reputation. Entertainers entertain. We entrance people, even when we act like fools. I am an entertainer. Period. It would harm my reputation as the Great Satriano."

"But you feel bad, Pietro. I can see it in your eyes, the eyes of a child."

"My eyes are the eyes of an entertainer, a cornetist. Bad publicity can be good."

"It can also be harmful."

"Whatever the consequences, I will remain the Great Satriano. What is it that Americans say, 'warts and all'?"

Musa, grabbing the newspaper with the jam stuck to it, reads the headline aloud, " 'Green Eyed Monster Strikes Denver City Band'…it was their turn to play their music. You played their song instead. Have you no shame? You should go to confession. Maybe Father Morscheni…"

"Father Morscheni knows nothing of music…"

"The people do not side with you. They felt bad for Anton Knoll and Marie McNell. They played the song eight different times to standing ovations. You are a fool! How could you act so childishly? It is only music. They respect you but you did not respect them."

As women so often experience, this is a time my husband needs his wife to act like a mama.

I look down. I feel like I am being scolded, and it makes me think of Mama. Mama would have taught me these things, would have lectured me at her knee, the same way Musa does.

Musa stops talking, and folds her hands on the table and looks like she has made her concluding arguments.

She is being reasonable, and I do not want to hurt her feelings, so I say softly, "Even after the music, I am an entertainer, and only secondly a man. I shall remain an eccentric entertainer. I will not apologize publically, but will send private letters to Signor Knoll and Signora McNell."

I squeeze my coffee cup hard, look at my musician hands, throw the paper on the floor, and walk to my study. The room is dark and cold, with only a small glimmer from the fire in the fireplace the night before. I hold the cornet for a long time in the dark embers of my study.

Then I hold it to my lips, for comfort.

Time passes. I review my actions the night before. It is a bit of a blur. To help me remember, I go to the kitchen and get the *Denver Times* and bring it back to my study. Sometimes it is hard to believe all these articles in the paper are about me. Sometimes it seems I am reading about another person. I stoke the fire, and the room brightens as the sun starts ascending on what is going to be a hot day.

Under the headline is a sub-headline, "Visiting Professional Cornetists Accuse Signor Pietro Satriano of Grave Breach of Courtesy." Then, beneath that, in an outlined box, is the following quote:

Professor Knoll's Protest

"Professor Satriano overstepped the bounds of professional courtesy in playing a cornet solo preceding us, but, as we are prepared to take care of ourselves in a musical way, perhaps there was no harm done. Nevertheless, we trust that it will not occur again. The duet, 'Quis

est Homo,' from the Sabat Mater *was played in an artistic manner.*
We believe that Signor Pietro Satriano will regret having allowed his
jealousy to overcome him."

I close my eyes. The memories are coming back about all the
events yesterday. I read on, even though it is embarrassing and
painful. I make a mental note to not give any more interviews to
the reporter who wrote the story.

Musical jealousy is playing havoc with the band at the City
Park, and serious disruption is impending. Last night band leader
Pietro Satriano overstepped the bounds of professional courtesy, say
his accusers, and three popular cornetists fell prey to the green-eyed
monster.

A.K. Knoll and Marie McNell, two famous cornetists and
composers, engaged at great expense to play for two weeks at City
Park, appeared on the program for the first time last night. There was
a large crowd drawn by the new attractions and classical night. The
interest of the evening naturally centered about the much-talked-of
performers. When the program announced that their time had come,
there was a hush of expectancy. Ms. McNell and Mr. Knoll, seated on
the bandstand, looked at Satriano, but Satriano was busily arranging
music. Before anyone knew just what was coming, Satriano stepped
forward and in another moment was playing a cornet solo. He fairly
threw himself into the music, and when he ceased there was a wild
burst of applause from the spectators. Ms. McNell and Mr. Knoll were
placed in a position that was helplessly awkward. They retreated to
the back of the grandstand and gazed out upon the water.

Before Satriano had finished his encore, the fact that he had
taken precedence to the strangers dawned upon the people—for the
attitude of the cornetists was visibly embarrassed. Satriano finished,
and a still more awkward silence ensued. For a moment Ms. McNell
and Mr. Knoll hesitated. Satriano turned to them with an air of
"Now beat me if you can," and Miss McNell stepped forward.

Eight times the visiting cornetists responded to encores, and every time Satriano grew more angry.

I put down the paper and rest my head on the fireplace mantel. Was it really that obvious I was so upset? I put my head in my lap, my hands over my head for a few minutes, and then resume reading this painful account. I will get even with this damned reporter.

Satriano is one of the most jealous musicians in Denver. Like Cavallo and all other popular musicians, he wants to be the people's favorite.

I smile. At least the reporter got one thing right.

"They talk about cornet kings and queens," said Satriano. "I'll show them myself. There's Bellstedt. They call him 'king,' and now here comes a 'queen.' I can beat all the kings and queens. You come out to the park tonight and I will show you who is king."

It was several hours before the concert that Satriano made this statement. He had evidently planned to meet and fight the enemy with his cornet. The result was far from what was expected.

"The Denver Times Two-Step" will be played for the first time tonight at the City Park. The two-step was composed by A.H. Knoll and dedicated to The Times.

I stand and pace the floor. How could they? Did *The Times* run this article to disrespect me? Did Mr. Knoll butter them up by dedicating the song to them? So much for objectivity in journalism. Maybe they bought their way into getting press. And to many people who do not know, I get stuck looking like a loose cannon and they get all the praise because they are victims.

Everyone has a place where they feel the most comfortable. For me, it is not the band shell, or the orchestra pit, walking in nature, or even my own bedroom. It is the piano bench. When I die, I would like to be composing at the piano, my last fermata still damp with ink. Fermatas sustain a note a little longer than normal; they briefly prolong a note. Many musical scores end with a fermata and I want my life to end accordingly; sustaining a few lingering seconds, those last breaths of air.

CHAPTER EIGHTEEN

"[His arms] reach out so far beyond the body
that one not accustomed to the acrobatic feats
of Denver's band master gasp…"

Pietro

I am walking home on Curtis Street. It rained during the performance. It used to be on Curtis Street there were horses all lined up at this time of night, people in the taverns and at the theatre, their horses tied up to posts, seemingly visiting with one another, anxious for their owners to reappear so they can move along and plod along day after day, like they always do, and like people do, really. But recently there are very few horses and more and more automobiles. One can tell which horses belong to musicians who play string instruments: their tails are barren, virtually missing.

I will have to get me an automobile. With my salary from the city for conducting, my weekend gigs at the Orpheum and Elitch Gardens, plus lessons, I have managed to piece together an income that will allow me to buy an automobile. I had never really thought of it seriously before now, but yes, it is time. I am one of the few musicians who still walks to the theatre, or takes the streetcar. I like to walk, but an automobile allows freedom, and it is the American way. It would probably take me only a few minutes to drive home, but it takes twenty minutes or so to walk.

As I think about this, I get that feeling that people get when someone is looking at them from behind. That feeling that one is being watched, being followed. But who would follow me? I am just a musician, a rather nice man, and a decent citizen, in spite of what my ex-wives think about me. Denver is a fairly safe place. I turn around and look, but all I see are the electric lights of the streets, the glistening from the rain on the automobiles. It must just be my imagination. Then I stop walking to see whether I can hear footsteps, but there are no footstep sounds. I see rats or mice in a trash bin, all excited about some great find. Maybe that is what I heard. Their eyes could have been following me.

Nonetheless, I walk home at a quickened pace, speed up my steps, my boots splashing the puddles somewhat. It seems as though I am stomping, as if in a march. Why am I walking fast in spite of the logic that no one is following me?

I worry that as one of the best-known Italian people in the state, there are people who would love to hang me; to make a spectacle of Signor Satriano.

I still think someone is following me.

Musa

Pietro came home with the most wonderful news last night: He wants to buy a motorcar! Most of our neighbors already have one. He is worried he will not be able to drive well. Sometimes he is very insecure. He would never tell the fellas he is afraid to drive, but he tells me. He crashes his bicycle sometimes, and I do not know why. It seems to me he would be a good driver, so well coordinated to play several musical instruments, but put him on a bicycle and he is "ass over teakettle" as he says. This sounds like one of his made up expressions, although I am unsure, maybe it is an old Italian expression. Maybe it is some kind of men talk, what they talk about when they drink gin at the bars.

There was something else about Pietro last night when he came in. He seemed a little shaken, a little nervous or something. He stood on the front porch for a long time, just looking around.

I went out to ask him what he was doing, and he said absently, "Just enjoying the nice evening" but really, it was cold and raining. I asked whether anything was wrong, and he said, "No, my love." Still, he was looking around, as if trying to find something, looking for someone. I went back into the house to complete some knitting. Carroll was already in bed.

He has not said one word about the aria I...helped him with.

Pietro came in and asked me if anything unusual happened that day; I said everything was normal. There were no phone calls, the milkman came by, the ice man brought us enough ice to last through the weekend, we received the new City Directory, and I cleaned the house, baked bread and read all day.

He didn't say much, but looked out the window and checked all the windows and doors in the house and went to bed.

I decide to call Hester on the telephone this morning and tell her I am concerned about Pietro.

Hester says, "What is it now? You tell me he is acting strange all the time, leading imaginary orchestras in the parlor, staying out late, staring into space, going into rages, and then being nice to you..."

"No, no...this is something new. I have never seen him nervous before."

She just goes on and on, telling me about how the streetcar may go out of business soon because of motorcars, and fewer people are attending operas because of picture shows. I hardly think this would make Pietro get nervous and lock the doors, which he seldom bothers to do; it is usually me. His mind is often elsewhere; his mind is in the world of music.

Pietro

On Saturday, Musa and I look at new automobiles. I know nothing about automobiles, but I talked about it with Frank Russomanno, Concetta's husband. The only kind of transportation I ever purchased was a horse. I am feeling a bit awkward. I put on my best suit, and Musa gets all dressed up and has her hair done for this special occasion, and Carroll comes with us and wears his best knickers.

I get in to what is called the driver's seat. I start the car, and the salesman says, "Put your foot on the accelerator," and I do, and we heave forward with a spurt and sputter. I pull the choke instead of the brake and we keep going. Musa grabs her hat, and Mr. Salesman —whatever his name is—says, "Whoaaaa," as if trying to command a horse. Eventually, I get the automobile to stop, just moments before we would have collided with the streetcar. That little scary moment makes everything seem even more fun.

I buy the automobile, and the family and I drive around Washington Park all day. We have so much fun. It is a beautiful fall day and life seems good. I could drive this into town tonight, have my own automobile waiting for me, and not have to walk or take the trolley. The thought of walking in town at night bothers me. Someone was following me; I just know it. But I suppose a person could follow me in an automobile, too.

Musa and I have the evening meal early, so I can get to the office before the concert at the Orpheum later tonight. "Goodbye, it has been a fun day," I say as I put on my coat and hat. "I'll be home around ten thirty."

Musa is worried about me driving the automobile at night. "Are you sure you have had enough experience driving? Maybe you should wait a few more days, or have Tony or Sal give you more driving lessons…"

"Musa, I'll be fine. Really."

I go to my office at Sixteenth Street. Violet, my secretary, is waiting for me. Violet, of course, does not work for me on Saturday nights. Violet and I started having an affair months ago. They say I am a ladies' man; I always have women around me. I do not try to attract them, they just flirt and cajole. In Italy, affairs are quite common. And, who am I to disappoint the young ladies?

I remember a poem written by James Joyce, that reminds me of Violet:

> The eyes that mock me sign the way
> Whereto I pass at eve of day.
>
> Grey way whose violet signals are
> The trysting and the twining star.
>
> Ah star of evil! Star of pain!
> Highhearted youth comes not again
>
> Nor old heart's wisdom yet to know
> The signs that mock me as I go.

Violet is dressed in her flowery dress that shows some of her calf; a proper lady would never wear a dress this high. The fellas at the Potenza Lodge and the fellas in the band all tease me; they know about me and Violet…and, some of the other women who have coveted me.

Violet is in quite a mood tonight. She kisses me excitedly when I walk in the door. She is wearing evening gloves, a large hat, and what is called lipstick; it makes her lips appear moist and red, like an open rose after a rain shower.

"Let's try out the Tin Lizzy! Come on, Pete, let's do a night on the town!" She is kissing me again, grabbing me. She makes me drop my hat.

"How about after the performance tonight? I can be with you for just a while. I am a married man, you know. I have to be careful; I cannot be seen driving around with a woman at night; it is improper."

"Your wife is very nice."

"Indeed; she is. I am torn because…"

Violet smiles innocently and deliciously, all at once.

"I will bring my new motor car around to get you here at about ten" I find myself saying.

I leave and proudly get into my Tin Lizzy and start the engine. It purrs at about a B flat. I park right in front of the Orpheum. A footman takes the automobile and parks it for me. "Nice set of wheels, Signor." I look over where the horses are, biding their time till their owners come out. I glance at the people coming to see me perform tonight, stepping off the streetcars, or parking their automobiles. The only thing perplexing is that people look angry when they drive, but then talk about how much fun it is to drive. Well, regardless, I can't help but feel a bit proud; that past, that reality of riding the streetcars has left me now. I will probably never ride a horse again. But some people think driving an automobile is a passing fancy, a phase.

All goes well at the Orpheum, the crowd is enthusiastic tonight. The people of Denver are very exacting in their musical tastes: we have to be spot on, or they will go to the picture show or the Tabor Opera House instead of seeing me. A few times during the performance I have passing thoughts of Violet…and Musa. Musa is safe; Violet is exciting, much like Anna was. Oh, if only I could keep myself from getting involved with wild women. We get a standing ovation again and again, and have to keep performing one encore after another. Finally, the curtain falls and I am able to leave. The footman brings my automobile around to the front. I wait, as if a maestro waiting for his carriage at La Scala, just as we used to do in Italy after a grand performance. Now, it is in style to drive oneself around town, but I rather miss not having a paid driver.

I drive a few blocks to my office on Sixteenth Street. Violet is there, looking ravishing. She must have just applied more of that lipstick because her lips look as red as a cherry tomato. I open the passenger door for her. She gets in, honks the horn. I tell her not to. We do not want to attract attention, I remind her. But there she is, pressing on the horn, shouting "Hey! Look at us." I am really getting too old to be with this type of woman. She has a bottle of gin, and we drink it down. I drive out near Washington Park and we stop for a while. We kiss in the car, and it brings back fond memories, like before I reached manhood and I would court a girl in a carriage. I notice the windows steaming up and wonder what I am supposed to do about this. We are…well, most of the way undressed, with these steamy windows and Violet's lipstick and her violet dress and all, and pooooffff…out of nowhere, through her side of the automobile…the flash of a camera. Dead on me.

Violet shrieks in delight and drinks more gin. "A picture of us indecent, what fun!"

Quickly, I put on my clothing, and wipe what is called the windshield with my coat sleeve and drive off to take Violet back to the office. Could it have been a reporter? What if it gets in the paper, and the rumor mill at the beauty parlor that Musa's family owns catches wind of it? Usually I dissuade her that the rumors she hears about me as the man about town are false, just rumors. But how much longer will she believe me, and can I keep this up?

Suddenly, I remember that I just learned how to drive this morning. I am driving in the dark and am unsure where all the streets are to get back to Sixteenth Street. Then, there is another automobile following closely behind. I am sure this must be improper etiquette but am uncertain how to tell someone behind me to not follow closely. The driver seems to want to get somewhere in a hurry. Well, I am a new driver, so I turn onto Seventeenth Street, hoping to make the driver happy, but the driver turns there also and follows me. Now I get worried. What if the man who took my photograph in that compromising position just moments ago is following me?

Just like last night, my heart beats fast, and I feel out of sorts. I do not see the fire hydrant on the sidewalk fast approaching, or the streetcar coming in the other direction, and I plow into both, "head on," as they say. It happens fast, but in slow motion time,

142 | Maestro Satriano

all at the same time, like at the picture show when the film suddenly breaks, and everything gets distorted and then stops in mid action. Or if I leave my phonographic records in the sun and play them on the phonograph when they have warped—it sounds slow, asynchronous, out of time, scary...too slow, too slow, my mind is thinking. Violet is lying in the street, but I am no longer associating red lipstick with Violet, but the gushing, spurting red blood of a ruptured artery. Papa saw this many times in the war, and how he described it seems to be what is happening to Violet. She looks beautiful, and even at this time I am aware my faculties have left me; but she does. My thought is: I have killed a beautiful person. Crimson, not violet, crimson, like wine...it is too much for my mind. And I in my new motorcar with a bump on my head, feeling strange, bleeding on my maestro coat.

I destroyed my automobile the day I bought it. I spend the night in the hospital with broken ribs, a concussion, and worst of all, my three middle fingers are broken on my right hand and my ring finger on my left hand, rendering it impossible for me to play musical instruments. I do not want to know if it will get better; I am too afraid to ask.

Violet is in a coma. She flew over the windshield and landed in the middle of Sixteenth Street. Photographs of me and Violet embracing in the front seat of my Model T, and then the fiasco downtown with the police and ambulance all around, appear on the front pages of all the newspapers, and stupor-like images of this play through my mind over and over as I am given morphine.

Understandably, Musa may never forgive me. She visits me in the hospital and says, "Pietro, I warned you! You should not have been out driving! You are not experienced enough to drive at night! And that woman!" She is always right, and I know it feels good to her to always be right, to be the one with better judgment and morals. Then she goes on, "You broke your left ring finger. Do you understand the symbolism there?"

I always tell her my usual spiel. "I am home with you almost all day; most men go off to work at an office or a factory. I sit in our parlor all day and compose, practice, or teach all day." I always told her Violet was my secretary, nothing more.

But there I am, my shirt off, the gin bottle on the floor, Violet's indecent undergarments being shown in the newspaper. Some of society thought it improper to publish the photograph of us. Though the talk of the town is, "That damn Italian finally gets what he deserves! He should know better. If he were a man of God and attended church, he would not be running around with young girls."

I feel shame. They are right about me. How could I give up my lovely wife and my professional reputation? I will have to go to court again. Mr. Habrl will be furious with me.

Musa visits me in the hospital again, but only to yell and cry. Tony and Sal and their wives, Annie and Lottie, visit. Their wives are distant and remote, and as women, they are not happy with my behavior. The morphine I was given for pain causes me to have strange dreams.

In one dream, I am a student again at the Royal Academy of Music. I am playing a grand old organ that is highly intricate and quite curious. A professor says to me, "You have not been playing your organ correctly for years." I try desperately to pull and push the right drawbars, but it only makes the sound worse.

"You have control over where you want the air to go, but your energy is going in the wrong direction." I am confused and ask questions about how to do that, but he is gone.

In another dream, my manhood is being chopped off and I am told it is for my own good. In my sleep, I shriek in pain. The nurse thinks I am screaming because of pain and brings more morphine.

In my delirium, I make a deal with God: I will be a better person, I swear, if only you let me live. If only Violet recovers and I can play music again, I swear, I will be an outstanding husband, father, and citizen. Please…I am a man, a man of sin at times, and supposedly God forgives those who believe in him.

The next afternoon, the doctor comes to tell me that I can go home, but advises not to drive for a while. I doubt Musa will let me drive for a long time. The insurance man comes to see me in the hospital. He is the only person who visits me and smiles. I hate insurance people; ones' misfortunes are his gain.

"Now, Pete, this here accident is going to cost you."

I just about jump out of bed and attack him, but I am becoming a better person. My fiery temper will be under control from now on. I do grimace in pain, kind of sneer at him, and he says, "Take the trolley, Pete; driving is not for everyone."

When I get home in the early evening, the house is dark. There are no lights on. Musa may be out shopping, or maybe Carroll has a ball game tonight, I think. I turn on one light, then another, and with each illumination, I am thinking I may suddenly see her, that the answer as to where my wife is will reveal itself with a flick of a modern switch. But as I pad around the house, there is no sign of Musa. I would think she would be here to take care of me, to fix me tea and nurse me back to health, but the other nagging thought is that I am undeserving of such a wife and she is right to leave me.

I walk into the kitchen, and switching on the new electric light does finally shed light on the mystery as to why my reliable wife is not home: she has left a letter on the table:

You are a good for nothing foolish man. When we married, you said you would change. You have caused disgrace for Carroll and me. I have moved back in with my mother. You ruined my trust in you.

I think there was more, but could not read it. Her words burn in my chest and feel like a hot fireplace poker sticking my broken ribs. She is right about me. I take my bruised body and lie down on the bed.

The next morning, it is a beautiful day. I awaken and look on Musa's side of the bed, but she is not there. Will she ever be there again?

I am starving and go to the kitchen. I realize there is no food in the house, and I have not had to cook in years, since Sal, Papa, and Tony and I lived in the little brick houses along the Platte River. We would make soup and simple things. I have become accustomed to better food now. I may have to eat like a pauper again, for all the money this accident is going to cost me.

I walk to the backyard and realize there is food to eat; it is autumn and the fall harvest is burgeoning. My tomatoes look ripe. I briefly think of Violet's lips, but turn my associations elsewhere, as I always will from now on.

In the pantry, I find macaroni, and proceed to make a dish I have not cooked in more than ten years: spaghetti! Ah, the comfort food of Italy. If ever I need comfort food, it is now. But do I deserve it? That is open for debate, I am willing to admit.

In Italy, a man has discreet affairs. We never had reporters following in automobiles, or even carriages. In America, there is less privacy, especially concerning indiscreet matters, which society seems to want to make public to punish people, in a puritanical way.

I stew the tomatoes and go to the garden to get some garlic. It feels good to be creating something other than music. I forget about my pain for a while, but when I feel the pain in my ribs again, I remind myself of the task at hand. I remember how Mama used to make spaghetti, and if she were here, that is what she would do to bring me back to health. Good spaghetti can cure the soul, she would say. Orsola makes spaghetti the way Mama used to, and her spaghetti is just as good. I should telephone her and tell her about my accident, but not about Musa or Violet. She will worry and be disappointed in me, as any older sister would be. Having a sister living at a distance, in Kansas City, has its advantages: Orsola only hears about the positive things; I send her newspaper clippings about my performances, but she really does not know entirely what I am up to here. I turn on the gramophone and listen to "The Entertainer."

It is hard to make spaghetti with four broken fingers, and even harder to do anything with a broken rib and a constant headache. Will I ever get better?

I lie down on the bed. Maybe Musa will never come back, and I will be in this house alone, lying in this bed, forever. I miss the sound of Musa prattling around in the kitchen, and of Carroll playing cowboys and Indians. Musa thinks I am oblivious to these things, but I am not. A musician is always listening.

More than anything, I am worried about Violet. Will she get better, or will she…die?

There is a knock at the door. I hobble out of bed; every step is hard. I look out the window and see a bald, middle-aged man I have never seen before. I open the door and the man says, "Herb Merwin, attorney at law."

I think, *damn*.

"Why are you here?"

"You have a legal problem and need a lawyer, son."

He is probably right, I do.

He tells me I have a mess on my hands, both personally and professionally. The City may put me on leave of absence from my contract, or I may be terminated completely. Violet and her family may sue. I will more than likely have to pay her medical bills. Musa is talking with an attorney about divorce and will say I am an unfit father.

He prattles on about other possible things that could happen, and possible remedies, but I am not entirely listening.

"How does such a talented man like you get into so much trouble?"

This snaps me back into active listening mode. I rather like this Mr. Merwin. Most people would not like an attorney at law who presents unexpectedly at one's doorstep soliciting business, but I have the feeling he is genuinely taking an interest in me.

"That's a good question. Women seem to get me into trouble. I think of myself as a good person though."

"Well, you are quite entertaining. You entertain the city of Denver with your antics on stage and off stage, and you have since your family came here."

I am not particularly happy to hear this.

"Your father was a drunk, then you divorced and married a fifteen-year-old girl. The divorce proceedings were in the paper. There are rumors you are a ladies' man, always entertaining ladies on the side. But then there are the good rumors, too, a royal musician, a bandmaster at a music conservatory in Milan at a young age, wonderful at teaching children. Paradoxes, Satriano. You are a man of paradoxes. Now, you buy a new automobile on Saturday morning, and wreck it with a floozy on Saturday night, and she is in a coma…Italians, Catholics…and you do not attend church…that does not look good, either. People wonder whether you are a heathen, a pagan, a devil worshiper. And then, that time there were visiting musicians and you could not control your jealousy and…"

"Please, Mr. Merwin, I do not need a lecture in my own home. Si, I am a colorful character." I put my head in my hands and close my eyes.

I feel like a bad child, like being scolded by the school principal for all my bad deeds. I look at my hands. I am determined that I must change, I must.

"Si, Mr. Merwin, please be my attorney. I need help."

"Hell no, son. I did not come over to represent you! I came over because you are one hell of a character. I just wanted to meet you and advise you to get an attorney. I would never take your case. You will never change. Representing you would be an ongoing saga. Oh, you'll be a big money maker for a fancy lawyer. Try Mr.

Teasdale or Mr. Harper, not me. I represent people whose cases I can win. Decent people who get into trouble."

Well, I am taken aback that he does not want to represent me and considers me to be indecent. I sigh and thank him for coming. I am a little confused; it is a bit unusual for an attorney to come to one's house unsolicited, but I am kind of an unusual man and bring unusual things upon myself, I am learning.

Just then, I smell something burning. Ah, the spaghetti! I hobble into the kitchen, lift the lid of the old pot pan. My spaghetti is burned. I turn off the stove, open up the windows to let the smoke out, and go back to bed.

I spend a lot of time in bed the next few days. There are knocks on the door and the phone rings a few times, but I do not answer. I am setting up a plan for how to deal with my problems and waiting for my body to heal.

I have lots of dreams. I realize that when I thought Musa had scolded me in the hospital about the accident, it was a dream. She left and I have not seen her since that fun day we bought the automobile and drove all over Denver.

I dream about Blackfoot. Blackfoot comes to town with his wife and son. He seems taller and bigger in town than he does at Garden of the Titans. He comes to my doorstep with them, looking so peaceful, his pipe in one pouch and his flute in another pouch. His wife has wildflowers around her neck and she takes them off and puts them around my neck. They just stand there and look at me, and they seem so calm. Blackfoot is looking at me; he seems so proud of his family. It seems like he is trying to convey something to me without speaking, but I do not know what it is. He seems content. I am thinking he is brave to come to town. Most men would run, hide, or get out their shot guns and shoot an Indian standing at one's doorstep. I am trying to figure out how he got to town so quietly and peacefully; why isn't he creating more of a ruckus?

I have never thought of it before, but Blackfoot, in many ways, is the person I respect the most. He has nothing to live for except today. He has no contracts to fulfill and no money he needs to earn. He is quiet, strong, gentle, and loves to play music. Then Blackfoot goes away; he and his family seem to be drifting backward, and they slowly disappear. I have several morphine-induced dreams like this over the next few days. It would not surprise me if Blackfoot really came. He has a quiet way of knowing. I think he may know I am in trouble, and may be trying to help in some otherworldly kind of way, if not literally trying to help in the real world.

After this last series of dreams, I awake with a start and sit bolt upright in bed.

Musa told me about a book she read that was written by a young, unusual doctor in Vienna, a Dr. Freud. Ah, Vienna, the operas and the coffee houses. I am unsurprised that a doctor in such an intellectual community started this new treatment. From what I hear, Dr. Freud based his theories on Wagner. Opera: the way to the soul.

The book says that dreams are important, like a window to the soul. I rummage through the house to see whether I can find it. It is a tome of a book, so it should not be too hard to find. While searching for it, it occurs to me that it must be very hard for Musa to find anything, even her own things, for all my musical scores take up so much room. Then, under some of Bach's "Preludes," I find it: *Interpretation of Dreams*. I spend the whole day reading through it: Dreams are wish fulfillment, we are what we are because we have been what we have been. Dreams are the royal road to the unconscious.

Musa told me that Freud called his treatment "the talking cure," and that people's problems can get better by talking about them. I think of Mama and Papa, who would talk to a priest in Italy when something was wrong. I thought they were going to ask for prayer or confession, but maybe just talking helped them? Papa did talk to Father Lepore a few times, and liked him. But Father Lepore has died, and I am afraid that if I walk into a church, it would crumble because of all my sins. I will see if there is one of these new kinds of doctors in Denver. Musa told me more: when people go to see Dr. Freud in Vienna, they lie on a divan and say whatever comes to mind first. It sounds like a parlor game.

I move all my music scores and lie down on the divan. I have never done this before, mostly because there is music in the way, but also because I am always composing and playing. The light is coming through the windows in a certain way, the way it does only in fall. This makes me miss Musa, because she is always moved by how the late afternoon sun shines through the west window, a deep warm orange tone inviting itself into our parlor, year after year, like a reliable friend who comes visiting the same time, in the same way, but it is only a brief prelude to winter, which reminds me of Vivaldi, and I will have to listen to him some afternoon soon.

So, if I were talking to Dr. Freud, my first thought would have been the sun and Musa. Hmmm…I am unable to divine much information from this, although maybe Dr. Freud could. So, I change position a bit, and try to clear my mind. I think about the Royal Academy of Music. There were some good experiences there and some bad. Just like me; I am both good and bad. Divorces, fighting, adultery, and one time I put putty in someone's horn to sabotage a performance so that I would win.

Actors pretend to be other people, but as a musician I can always be myself, but I think musicians will more and more have to be actors because of moving pictures. Once sound and images can be synchronized, it will open up a different world for entertainment in general, but especially for musicians.

To try to imitate what I would really get if I were in Dr. Freud's office, I say those things not to myself, but out loud. I talk to myself until the sun's rays have departed my home and now are likely visiting other neighbors.

I call the hospital and ask how Violet Tarno is. They tell me she was discharged this morning. I am so relieved. I do not identify myself to the person who answered the telephone, but after the message is conveyed, the person says, "Thank you for calling, Mr. Satriano." I look at the receiver in amazement and hang up the phone.

I could still be sued, but at least she did not die. I phone the florist shop and request flowers be sent to her home. I would buy her flowers and bring them to her, but it might be uncomfortable for her and I do not want her, or anyone else, to think I am still courting her. Common sense tells me that I should not have any contact with her. I will not continue to court women. Period. Basta, Pietro! Basta! I tell myself.

Then I have another idea. I have not reached out to Musa. I figured she wanted distance, but maybe she does not. Maybe she wants me to visit. I do miss Carroll, the sound of him in the house, the laughter of children. I call the florist again. Florists must know everyone's business in town. I tell her the card should say, "Musa, please come back to me. Come live with me. I am sorry. Carroll, Papa loves you and misses you."

The florist must be a real professional, for she does not comment, but I bet as soon as she can, she tells her friends and family and calls society all over Denver to tell them of my sentiments and gossip; oh the gossip. They are probably saying I am living with a three-legged circus lady who weighs three hundred pounds and she is pregnant with my child, and we have one child together who has three legs and plays the cornet and is a child prodigy like me, and if only it weren't for those three legs...

I bathe and dress. It is the first time I have really gotten dressed and gone anywhere since the accident. I walk down the street gingerly, as my ribs still hurt. I am feeling better, and tip my hat when a lady approaches me on the street; my manners deteriorated for a while after the accident. It hurts me to see automobiles; I owned one for a day and wrecked it and almost killed myself and another person. I go to Mt. Carmel Church, where Papa would go sometimes. Sal and Tony and I still talk about Father Lepore.

I walk in and there is Father Morscheni, talking to an altar boy.

"Father, have you time to hear my confession?"

"I have been expecting you."

There is a long pause and we look at each other. He has been expecting me? I shrug my shoulders and say, "Well?"

"You are not a member of this church. You have sinned and are an ex-communicated Catholic."

"Yes, but every man is a sinner."

"Indeed. If you are willing to give a true confession, I can make suggestions and ask God to watch over you."

He seems to acquiesce, and he may have smiled, but I do not know. Maybe he winced. We go into the tiny cubicle and I open the little curtain. Memories from being a boy and going to confession with Mama and Papa feel palpable in the tiny little space, years and miles away from Italy.

I tell Father Morscheni everything—about my affairs, my temper, my lies, my misdeeds as a husband, my rampages as a performer, my jealousy.

There is a long silence. I am getting worried Father Morscheni has fallen asleep, or is it just like what everyone else thinks about me? Is he sitting there thinking I am quite a character, or is he thinking there are no prayers that can absolve my sins and I will be in purgatory forever?

"Father?"

He begins speaking in Italian to me; why, I do not know. "Pietro, do you see why your wife views you as a *menefreghista*?"

I have not thought of that word in years. *Menefreghista* refers to a person who is careless or does not care.

"Si, Father, I can."

"Avoid the things you want to avoid. Think of God."

I hear him get up from the small wooden bench and leave the room. I listen to his footsteps walk out of the sanctuary. It seems important to do this.

Then, I, too, leave the sanctuary. I can hear my own footsteps well; the acoustics in churches are wonderful.

I am surprised by his advice; I thought he would tell me to say twenty-five Hail Mary's for three days, or say other specific prayers. Instead, he gives me practical advice.

A day of confession and introspection seems to lighten me. I feel lighter. Between Dr. Freud and confession, which I now see those lines are very blurred, I am feeling like I really could become a better person.

It has been a few days since I sent flowers to Musa and Violet, and I have not heard from either of them. I must be content with the way things are, for I cannot change them.

At least I am feeling physically better now. I am in the process of moving all of my sheet music to my office. I should not have left it here, just piling up year after year. No wonder Musa complains. It is being hauled off into a horse-drawn wagon. I have told myself I can have no more than fifty scores in the house at one time. I am wearing old clothes, my dungarees, and so is the man helping me, an old gypsy who rides his wagon up and down the streets, looking for odd jobs to help people and earn money. I hand the music to him out the front door, and he puts it in the wagon. Some of the music belonged to Papa, and came over with him on the ship. When he was in New York City and came back for us, he wrote in advance, "Could you please find all of my Wagner scores and pack them for the voyage?" Our suitcases were full of music; we had more music than clothes.

I tell the gypsy to be careful, be careful now; this sheet music is really old. Indeed, it has a musty smell and the paper is very thin and disappearing. A lot of it is torn, almost shredding. A lot of the music has stains on it, but it is not *caffe* stains, which is so often the case with my own music. Instead, there are many reddish spots; the unmistakable stamp of Papa's sheet music: wine stains.

I hand the gypsy another thirty scores out the door. I am holding them in my left hand, but looking toward the kitchen. "Be careful with these..." but he does not take them from my hand. I turn to see why he is not reaching for them, and...there is Musa.

She very curtly says she has to get more clothes for herself and Carroll. I try to talk to her, but she moves around the house quickly, not wanting to talk and barely looking at me.

I understand and give up. I sit on the divan and let her do what she needs to do. The gypsy looks at me sympathetically.

CHAPTER NINETEEN

Laws, honey, don' yo tell me nuffin 'bout yo ragtime!

Look at dat fella!

I golly, he feet move lak de constable

wid a warrant fo chicken stealin'!

Go along dar, don' yo tell me nuffn'!

Pietro

Snow fell last night, an early, autumnal snow. Its whiteness obliterates everything else, and the return of coldness is welcomed after an unusually warm summer.

With these thoughts, I put on my heavy coat and gloves and go out to retrieve the newspaper. The paper is difficult to find, as the paperboy apparently threw it before the snow began to fall. I am always anxious to find the paper because it is the main way I learn about myself; that is, of the public's opinions and rumors about me. It never really occurred to me that I would be a public person. I just set out to be a musician, but the newspapers in America read like gossip columns.

I get my shovel and dig around where the paperboy usually throws the paper: upper right side of the front stoop, generally aimed directly at Musa's rose bushes. I lift up a heavy heap of fluffy snow and find a small wooden figurine. I examine it closely, my spectacles fogged up due to the rare humidity in the air. I hold it to my nose to examine it; it is carved and appears to be an animal shape…Blackfoot's amulet! I cannot believe it; he really was here!

It was not a dream. He came here, right into the city proper, and left something he is always carrying with him; it must be something important to him, the equivalent of a rabbit's foot, I think.

I need to think about this further, so I quickly return to the warm house, with my newspaper and amulet. The house is quiet, painfully so, and it makes me think about how Saturday mornings usually were when Musa and Carroll were home. Musa would make pancakes for breakfast and listen to music on the gramophone. In the morning, she would bake bread for the weekend, and the aroma would permeate the house, just like a delightful sonata. Carroll would be out playing in the snow right now, or his friends would be here and they would be throwing a ball around the house and Musa would be telling them to "take it outside," sounding more like a bouncer than a mother.

I have to focus extra hard on reading the news this morning, because I am excited that Blackfoot was here, but my mind needs to settle down before I think about it. I put the amulet in my pocket, so that I will not sit and think about it. I forge ahead, reading the paper and eating my toast.

Then I look at the mail, something I used to do every day, but I do not keep a regular schedule anymore. There is a letter from my attorney, Mr. Teasdale. It states that Miss Violet Tarno will not sue me, but I must pay her medical bills. That is good news, and I am fully prepared to do so.

In order to pay for Violet's medical bills, I rummage through the closet and take out a gold medallion that I received in 1902, when my band won First Place at a competition in Salt Lake City. The city of Denver gave it to me as an honorary gift after we won, and it cost $250. I will still have money left over after I pay, and I will save that money, and will not have to spend the rest because of my foolishness ever again.

I wonder what Carroll and Musa are doing today?

Carroll plays with soldiers and rides a bicycle. Brahms loved toy soldiers. I played soldiers when I was a boy, but did not have a bicycle. We did not have those when I was a boy; what the modern age allows these days is extraordinary. When he was younger, I gave him a teddy bear and told him that it was named after President Teddy Roosevelt and that I performed for him several times, and he seemed unimpressed. It is hard to relate to him, hard to understand him at times. When I was his age, I was always practicing cornet; I seldom had time to play games, and Carroll has so much more, but seems indifferent to me and ungrateful and unappreciative of me; but he is young yet.

I do more thinking than reading the paper today. Blackfoot was here? How would he know where I live? Did he follow me here? Does he read and I am unaware of it? Some people say Indians have heightened senses and can hear and smell better than other people. Did he smell me, or commune with the Gods to get here? I am just baffled. I hope he made it out of town safely and is back up at Garden of the Titans. I look outside at the snow and do not see any prints on our sidewalk. Maybe the rabbit's foot has been there for weeks, and I just did not see it. No one else seems to take much of an interest in me. Oh, Sal's wife brought over some chicken soup a few days ago, and she cleaned up the kitchen for me. My brothers are staying away, keeping a distance from me. The men in the band and Mr. Habrl have not visited, but of course I have not been to Luigi's. It would be nice to visit the fellas and play poker, but what will that really do for me?

I walk outside and look out at the blanket of snow and look to the west, toward Garden of the Titans. I have an idea that might help me. Lying on the couch is helping, but there may be something that will help me even more.

Am I going crazy, or have I been *pazzo* all along and am about to make a sharp turn toward normalcy, or health, or enlightenment? I am excited and anxious to find out.

CHAPTER TWENTY

Society drives out every afternoon to hear him
and goes home with his pleasant toot doing a
reverberation act in society's car—viva la Satriano

Pietro

I put on my heavy coat, hat, mittens, and snowshoes, and bring a change of clothes and lots of sweaters and blankets. I take the streetcar to the very last stop before I head up to the little town near Garden of the Titans, called Morrison.

There is hardly anyone on the streetcar today; Denver is buried under a record snowfall and everyone is staying home, except me: I am walking to Garden of the Titans to see my friend, Blackfoot. The streetcars will stop running in an hour or two, for the first time ever. The snow does not bother me; I just feel drawn, no...led...to go to Garden of the Titans, now, to see Blackfoot. I do not exactly know why.

There is less snow out to the west, I think because it is a sunny day and there are no trees up here; it is mostly desert-like. The streetcar conductor looked at me rather strangely when he saw my suitcase, and I said I was going to Garden of the Titans. I was raised in a large city, Naples, then moved to Milan. I became a country boy, or a mountain man, according to some, after moving to Denver, but still, I am a city person, even though Denver is a small city. I was worried the snow would be too deep to ride a horse, and how many people ride horses anymore? I am sinking in the snow, and it is up to my knees at times, but I keep going. I am walking alone in the snow to see a person who does not speak English, has never held a job a day in his life, has never ridden a streetcar or heard an orchestra play or been to Italy or eaten spaghetti, but something makes me keep walking.

Hours go by and I can see the red rocks, looming above me, their crevices and tops lined with snow. I am freezing, but enchanted by the beauty. I keep walking.

When it is dark, I reach Garden of the Titans. I have never slept outside in my life. In Italy, if you sleep outside, you are poor. I pull out Carroll's tent and set it up. We bought him a tent so that he could go camping with a new organization, the Boy Scouts of America, it is called. I pull out a stove to warm up some spaghetti I brought with me. Other sensible people wisely decided to stay home tonight, and are gathered around their hearths, or are putting more coal in the furnace, but for unknown reasons, I am lying in snow in a remote place.

These cliffs have provided protection from the elements for the native people for centuries. Now I, too, am here to be protected from the elements, or perhaps from my own elements.

It is dark and the stars are beautiful. I have nothing to do and nowhere to be, and I start composing a symphony in my mind. I should have brought my composition books; the stars seem like conductors, orchestrating a silent symphony above my head. In thinking about this, many things are over my head and out of my reach these days, including my life. I fall asleep pretending the stars are performing for me, and I am the silent, omniscient moon, watching the excited stars twinkle. There is a myth that Vega, one of the brightest stars in the sky, is a lyre, or a harp, that was played by Orpheus, who was murdered. Zeus saw to it that he and his harp were placed in the sky for eternity, to make music.

There is a lyre on Papa's headstone at Fairmount Cemetery to signify to all who walk by on the little dirt path that he was a man of music, to signify his belief, or hope, that he is—or was, or would be—like Orpheus.

I hear snow falling off the rocks at times and icicles crashing off the side of cliffs in the middle of the night. I hear large animals tromping along through the snow. I do not care to look and see which animals they are; I do not want to know that bears and mountain lions are probably watching me intently, wanting to pounce on this fella who has some unusual-smelling food. I am enjoying the night sounds. Maybe the night sounds will heal me.

Why is it I am a known musician? It all started with the cornet. But what is really special about playing the cornet? I know how to blow into a hollow tube that vibrates at a certain frequency.

What will I do if I am not a musician, and am again divorced? Where would I go, what would I do? I have fond memories of Salt Lake City, where my band came in first place in a national competition. I have family in Kansas City; I could live with Orsola. I think maybe it would be fun to ride the rails and be a hobo, or a train conductor. Could I really keep myself from being a musician, from blowing into a hollow tube and waving a baton for a living? If I did work on a train, I could play "Sleeper's Wake" in the morning, and help lull the passengers to sleep at night with my gentle violin or the soothing strains of my cornet playing "Holy City." But what if I could not work as a musician, could I be a dishwasher or a porter? I would probably be happy, as long as I could play music.

The next morning, I awake with a start. I hear something walking through the snow at a fast pace. Then the footsteps stop. I put on my spectacles and see Blackfoot, who apparently just killed a deer with a bow and arrow, and he is skinning it with a tool that looks primitive. He glides the tool over the carcass with finesse, as if cleaning a musical instrument. At times, he seems to scrub a bone, and it looks the same as when Musa scrubs the dinner dishes.

I want to talk to him, and he sees that I am awake and walks over to me. Why do Indians never smile? I take it he is happy to see me, but he stands over me, looking at me with his usual, rather serious, facial expression.

I awkwardly stand up. I have to start communicating with him somehow, and I now know that he probably knows more than he lets on. I say, "Thank you for coming to my house. How did you know something was wrong? Thank you for the amulet." I hand it back to him.

Then, I see him smile for the first time. He gently takes my arm and puts the amulet in my coat pocket.

I point to my chest and say, "Pietro, I am Pietro."

He touches his chest and says, "Pietro."

"No, no, I Pietro." I pound my chest more adamantly.

He points to his chest and says, "Blackfoot."

I smile and shake my head. "Good!"

"Good!" he repeats, and points to his chest.

He starts to walk away, then looks back to see whether I am following him. I get the idea and follow him, after picking up my meager belongings. We walk for hours, over the ridges of the red rocks into an area of pines, and nothing but pines.

There are other Indians gathered around tipis and mud houses built low to the ground. There are three women and four children. One girl, about four years old, cannot walk. Her leg is deformed and appears to be too short, and her upper lip is barely there. A woman smiles at me. Apparently Indian people do smile. Blackfoot and I sit and the women bring us some kind of tea, and a type of bread that has agave for flavoring. Agave is popular in Denver as well. After the meal, all of us walk even further into the woods, the little girl with the deformed leg hobbling along, leaning against others. We stop at a Ponderosa pine tree that is convoluted. It twists at its base, then twists again, the same direction. The tree seems to be diseased, and I'm unsure why we are all gathered around it.

SIGNOR SATRIANO MISSING

No one has seen Signor Satriano in approximately two weeks. Authority has it he may have left town due to financial and legal problems. He was placed on leave after an automobile accident and indecent photos were published in a local paper.

There are abundant rumors that he may have gone to Los Angeles, where his second wife, Anna, is an opera singer. Others are worried he may be ill or may have wandered off during last week's snowstorm.

Some of society is happy Signor Satriano has left town, and some people genuinely miss him. "He represented our city as a musical center all over the country and the world." Another woman said, "There was never a man more charming, talented and enigmatic than Professor Satriano, who graced our fine city with music, mirth and excitement from the day he arrived." Many people think it is a bad omen that he has disappeared without a trace. A streetcar conductor said that during last Saturday's snowstorm, he was on the streetcar with a suitcase, and said he was going camping at Garden of the Titans. "If this is true, he may have had a nervous breakdown. Please call Denver Police if you see Signor Satriano or have any news as to his whereabouts," said Police Chief Robert O'Malley.

Pietro

The women dance and chant something. They dance in a circle, around the tree, and touch the tree four times each during the song. I cannot understand their words, but I hear the name "Pietro" and what sounds like "Wakan Tanka" over and over again. I am given bark to eat, the inside part, and it tastes soft and sweet.

Nightfall comes and everyone seems happy. The children play for hours together without fighting. Blackfoot is gentle with the women there, and attentive. We eat what I believe to be elk meat, and I am given a bowl of something to drink. Everyone gathers around me. I wonder why, but do not question it. I take one sip and stop, thinking that maybe I should pass it around, but the child who is so malformed brings the bowl back to my lips, and I drink the whole thing. Do they think I am sick? The women beat on drums that look very old and have animal skin pulled tight over them. They all look at me for a while, then I feel sleepy and have strange dreams. In my dreams, Blackfoot speaks English (if it is my dream, why does he not speak Italian?) and says to me, "The tree will hold your prayers for eight hundred years, and every wind will bring your prayers new breath."

This was the best part of the dream, or whatever it is I am experiencing. After this, though, a bear is chasing me, and Blackfoot cuts two holes in my chest, over by the prayer tree. In my nightmares, Carroll, Violet and Musa die. Coyotes come up to me and seem like friendly dogs and sit in my lap, but then turn on me. Then the bear comes back and saves me. All these images come to me and seem very real, as if a lifetime of intense events are happening in a short period of time. Mama comes to me; she says, "Pietro, be a good boy, go back to your home and be a husband and father." Then Papa appears to be spinning in the air and says, "Be a good musician, too," and he laughs and laughs and spins around in the air. Professor Romano comes to me. I cry and cry. "Pietro, music is also a type of mistress that can lead you astray..." and he floats away in the rocking chair he always sat in. I am frustrated I do not hear the rest of what he was saying. There is suddenly a child calling my name. It is Carroll, in the distance. He is a little boy, four or five. He says, "Papa, Papa, come play with me..." He has a ball in his hand. I want to run and hug my little boy, and play ball with him...I am running toward him, almost there, my arm now reaching out to touch him. I am inches away from him, just ready to touch him, and...suddenly I am on the old French ship again, trying to cross the Atlantic in that storm we went through. The ship is tilting, leaning, seemingly chopping through waves that threaten to completely encompass her.

I think there was more, but fortunately I awake. It is morning, and Blackfoot and his family are all standing around me, silent. I am very hot, but there is snow on the ground. I must have a fever. They nurse me for a few days, I think, and then I am better. Blackfoot and I smoke a pipe, then he hands me a flute made of an animal's bones. Blackfoot is playing the one I have seen him with before; it is made of cedar. I admire the flute; it would take amazing craftsmanship to make this with the primitive tools they have, probably years. I blow into it and it is a pleasant sound. It is a five-hole flute in the minor pentatonic scale. Then Blackfoot blows the same note, approximately a C2. Blackfoot seems to play whimsically, and we mimic each other playfully, and sometimes laugh.

The next day, it is sunny again, and it feels like it is time for me to leave. They are gathered around looking at me, and I take it they think it is time for me to leave as well. Something happened while I was with them; I changed. I wish I could give them something back; but I do not know what it would be. I was like a houseguest who came unexpectedly, got very ill, slept a lot, probably screamed in my dreams, ate their food, played their flutes, and left. They stand in a circle around me. The children touch me, the woman who seems to be Blackfoot's wife puts a bone necklace around my neck, and Blackfoot hugs me. Other than Papa and Professor Romano, he is the only other man who ever hugged me. Blackfoot takes me back to the place where I camped by myself that first night. There is still snow on the ground, and the sun is so bright against the snow I can barely see. I bow to him before I leave. I have bowed many times during musical performances, and I would bow in the presence of royalty when I was the musician for King Alphonso of Spain.

But today I bow to Blackfoot out of utmost respect, and turn and walk away.

Blackfoot just stands there, watching me leave. Every few minutes, I turn around to see if he is still there, and he is. At times I want to run back to him; he seems to care about me, and I do not know why. He just stands motionless watching me, the way a long-time caring friend or parent would watch someone leave, out of respect and love for someone traveling on a long journey. I start feeling teary eyed, knowing that he will watch me until I disappear into the horizon.

I make my descent out of the Garden of the Titans, back to the land where time is significant and there is a set pace to most endeavors, and language, rather than dreams and silence, rules our lives. Where the pulse is on the beat of time, and staccato sixteenth notes steal time.

CHAPTER TWENTY-TWO

There is expression and soul in Satriano's
playing. The horn when placed to his lips,
comes alive and is a thing of beauty.

The streetcar conductor seems very curious about where I have been and is surprised to see me again. "It was two weeks ago that you left; I dropped you off at the last stop out of town during a blizzard."

"That was two weeks ago? I thought I was gone for only a few nights."

"Everyone has been looking for you. Are you okay?"

"I am fine."

"Why didn't you tell us where you were going?"

"I did not think anyone really cared or would notice I was gone."

Then it occurs to me: I had an experience like Dante's *Inferno* in the *Divine Comedy*. Dante goes to hell, is cleansed of the seven deadly sins, of which some of them are lust and greed. Also like me, this happens when he is middle aged, which I am also. My rescuer's name is Blackfoot, but for Dante, it was Virgil who met him in a dark wood, and they went on an underworld journey together. As I ride the streetcar back to the center of Denver, I remember more about *The Inferno*. The psychics had to walk with their heads backward because of their sin of being able to see the future. Orsola would love this!

At my home, there are people gathered around, standing outside wearing coats. Mr. Habrl, neighbors, Tony and Sal and their wives. "Pietro! Pete!" I hear people calling me and everyone runs up to me. Most are smiling, but some look quizzical.

It is cold, and I invite everyone in. They tell me how worried they were, some people thought I had lost possession of my faculties, some thought I went to California, and some wondered if marital difficulties and losing my job…made me have dark thoughts.

"I am fine, really. I went to visit friends who live near Morrison." Everyone briefly looks at me kind of strange, but then go on talking. A policeman comes by to talk to me. I assure him I am fine. Lottie, Sal's wife, makes coffee for everyone and we talk and eat cake.

Mr. Habrl comes over to me. He lights a cigar and says the City of Denver wants to reinstate my contract. I am so happy, it feels like a holiday. Except, of course, my wife and son are not here…

"Yes! Yes! I want to be the people's musician again, but I will have to be the people's conductor from now on. Conducting only."

"The people of Denver love you. Everyone was worried. The head of City Council telephoned me and said, 'If we ever find him again, reinstate his contract.' I think he felt guilty."

I will meet with my band tomorrow and we can start rehearsals again soon.

I had no idea so many people cared about me. Life is big at times, then tiny, then scary, then dull, then rich, then unfair, then it all changes again in different mosaic patterns that makes it always interesting.

And no matter what, I always come back to music, to my prancing on stage, long intervals of times on the piano or blowing into my cornet, or sliding the bow over the violin strings.

It always comes back to music.

Musa

All over town, the word is Pietro has been found.

I quickly walk to our home on Ogden Street. It is autumn now, and I have been gone for three months. Yellow and orange leaves blanket the front yard.

I enter through the kitchen door, and the house is quiet, except I hear Pietro talking to someone. Is he talking to someone on the telephone? The kitchen brings back memories of living with Pietro; the mild aroma of garlic and sweet basil.

I walk into the living room, the modern term for parlor, which he calls his studio. I peer around the corner, and he is lying on the divan, talking to himself.

"Dr. Freud, it does seem that I have changed. I keep thinking of that poor Indian child with the deformed leg and lip. I wish that she could come to my concerts at Elitch's like other children, and that I could take her to a doctor, but it does not seem like there is anything that can be done. I miss Musa and Carroll…"

"I may be a fool of a woman," I interrupt him, "but I, too, have missed you."

He springs up from the divan and looks so surprised, and a bit embarrassed. I sit next to him on the divan, and realize the room is clean, almost spotless: there are no musical scores. He sees me looking around the room and knows what I am thinking. He takes my hands in his.

"I knew you were a womanizer when I met you. I knew you would be difficult to live with, but I thought I could put up with your shenanigans, because deep down you are a good, talented person, and even loyal, in your own way. I, too, am loyal, and against my better judgment, have decided to live out the rest of my days with you. I have no desire to be a divorced woman; the scorn of divorce is even worse for a woman than it is for a man. And Carroll, think of Carroll…"

Pietro kisses my hands and looks into my eyes in a way I have not seen since we were courting. But I look at his fingers on his hands, and they are crooked and bruised.

"Musa, I will not be able to play music as well as I once did. I can play the trumpet and cornet with my left hand, but not very well. My middle three fingers on my right and left ring finger were damaged in the accident. Playing piano or organ professionally will not be possible. I will have surgery next week, but the doctor is not optimistic."

I cannot believe he is handling this so well. He seems solemn and resigned to this news. And, he was always so careful about his hands. He shows me that he cannot bend his fingers or fully extend them.

Then, looking at me with his big brown eyes, more lovingly than he has in years, "I cannot thank you enough for fixing that aria I was working on years ago. You saved me. It was hard for me then to pay you a compliment, and to acknowledge your musical talent. I want you to play piano more, and be a musical person, too."

I had wondered for years why he never said anything about this. He had to have noticed. I am about to say more, but he seems intent to talk:

"Also, I need to tell you something about Violet, my former secretary."

I feel tense just hearing her name. He tells me how they met.

"I will still be able to conduct, compose and teach, and perform at small venues, like for children, but no more concerts. In a way, it is a relief. I have felt more peaceful without the demands of performing. I would do two concerts in the park, then sometimes at the Orpheum or the Tabor Opera House, and then occasional performances like the inauguration of the mayor, two or three concerts a day, ad nauseam, ad infinitum. It is time for me to start anew."

"How so?"

"You will see," he says, still looking at me and holding my hand.

"Our problems are not entirely you. It is me, too. I felt intimidated by you. I have made the mistake of idolizing you, thinking of myself as married to an entertainer, and not to a man who is my husband. You are my husband. This part of things is my mistake; it kept us distant. I will not do that anymore."

Tearfully, he seems to sincerely thank me. "But inasmuch as you have reason to apologize, I have as much or more reason to apologize."

I say, "Something has been missing from our marriage, and maybe it has been me, too, and not just you."

I will never forget that moment.

CHAPTER TWENTY-THREE

"Mr. Satriano is commended by musical authority
as the greatest band leader in the country."

Pietro

I feel that Musa reveals herself slowly to me, like music does, revealing herself to me over time. Or is it I who only notice her, incrementally, as I am ready?

It is a clear spring morning. Musa, Carroll, and I are all living together again, and I appreciate the family ties more. Later today, Carroll is going to play baseball after school, and I will be there to watch his game for the first time.

I am walking from my house to a new hospital that is only a few blocks from my home on Bell Avenue...ah, excuse me...the name of the street was changed to Ogden Avenue just recently. The new hospital is a children's hospital, and I never really thought of it until recently, but decided I would like to do some concerts for the children. I used to think teaching and performing for children was the lowest a musician could do, but have come to feel differently about this.

I walk a few blocks to Downing Street, where there is a large brownstone building. I enter and my heart beats as if following a measure of dotted quarter notes. There are children in wheelchairs, children without legs, children stricken with polio and tuberculosis.

I have gotten calls from the hospital over the years to perform. I was always busy and thought it would be beneath me; yes, the new Pietro admits these things to himself. The other reason is that I, like most other people, try to avoid suffering and seeing the plight of the poor and sick.

I talk to an administrator, a nice lady who is a nurse. "Signor Satriano, a pleasure to make your acquaintance. Please be seated." She is smiling and seems very accommodating. "My, the Maestro himself here at our children's sanatorium!"

I sit down in an old wooden chair that was meant for children, which many people would joke was just the right size for me. "I would like to do some concerts for the children. I would like to come on a regular basis and bring some joy here. Children are a delightful audience, easy to please."

"Signor, I have been calling you for years, and so did Mother Cabrini. Why did you decide to come now?"

I take out my cigar and start to light it, but the nurse shakes her head, so I put it back in my pocket, reluctantly.

"I have not told a story without a cigar for a long time. Well, I remember what it is like to be institutionalized. I was placed in an institution not because of a problem, but because of my talent. My talent caused me to have to live without my family and among strangers, much the way the children here do, who have leprosy and tuberculosis. I felt like I was trapped, and had the equivalent of some type of disease: but the focus was on my talent. No one ever told me I would fail. They just told me how great I was. I missed my family terribly. The focus was on me as a musician, and not as a person." I put my hand over my heart, feeling emotional. "Not once was it me, it was my talent, and that made me angry."

"So you feel like you can identify with the children here?"

"Si. I would like to come on a regular basis and perform. Sometimes by myself and sometimes with my students."

"Please, the children would love that, and it sounds like that would be good for you, too."

"Indeed. I have another question for you. I know of an Indian child, a young girl from a nice Ute family, who needs medical treatment. Please, is there anyone who can help her? If I get her here…"

"I am sorry, Maestro…we cannot take them in. If she is brought here and improves, she will be sent to a special school to learn to live in the modern world, and not the old ways of her heritage. It is sad for Native children to leave their families. Eventually, she will probably be captured and brought to a school anyway."

"Or she may die soon."

"I am sorry, but you might talk to Mother Cabrini about it."

"Thank you for your thoughts on this."

I put on my hat and walk toward the door. The nurse pulls something out of her drawer, ah, it is a photo of me, one of my early photographs, the one that was for sale in the photograph stores, and it used to say, "Here is Signor Satriano in the Fullest Kind of Action."

"Could you sign this for me, Signor?" she says shyly.

"Of course. No one has asked me for an autograph in years." She hands me the fountain pen, and I write, in what people tell me is a very artistic signature, "P. Satriano."

I walk out the door, into a warm summer day. She is right; I do not know why I did not think of it sooner. Mother Cabrini is the person to ask. She could help get the girl to a doctor, or she may be able to heal her and restore her health through prayer. There are stories that she has healed the sick and she could be made a saint someday. She is known as a dear friend to the Italian immigrants.

I get my old violin out of the cellar. I gave it to my manager, Mr. Habrl, for years so that Papa would not sell it. I have not played it in a long time. The truth is, the violin is my favorite instrument. Papa was a cornet player, so I became a cornetist also. For years I told myself I loved the cornet, and to some extent I do, but really, the violin is the sweetest, most angelic instrument, except that my hobbled fingers cause me to screech now, as if I am a beginner.

I had to earn a living, and there was more of a need for brass instrument music in the modern age than for violin, so it was also logical to play cornet and be a brass and wind bandmaster.

Musa

Pietro seems more relaxed since he disappeared during a snowstorm and has these unusual conversations on the couch with Dr. Freud. He performs for children at Elitch Gardens, and at the new children's hospital, and teaches Boy Scouts; it all seems to make him so happy. Children bring out the best in him, his gentleness and his playfulness, so buried for so many years. He smiles more, and I, too, am happier. We have come to think of working with children as his strength.

It is opening day at Elitch Gardens and I attend the festivities because Pietro will be performing. The flowers are blooming. I stroll around with my parasol and see Pietro from afar. He is walking around with young children. There is always a graceful rhythm to his stride. He helps a girl get on the carousal. He reaches into his pocket, the same pocket he keeps his pocket watch in, and gives the children candy. One boy falls and scrapes his knee, and Pietro gets down on his knees to console him. He tells the children to close their eyes and imagine they are in Africa. Then he blows a few notes on his trumpet, and says, "the elephants are coming!" He teaches them how to do the cakewalk. He always makes sure to include the children who have dark skin, as he is sensitive to unfair treatment of people because of their skin color. Maybe because he has traveled so much, and experienced this himself…

Part Three
1945–1946

CHAPTER TWENTY-FOUR

"I never try to control myself when leading the band."

Pietro

It is a beautiful day and I take a walk. My friend Luigi, who owns the shoe shop, has decided to open a restaurant next door to it. The talk here in the Italian colony is: What will the sign say in his window? The "Don't Go Elsewhere" sign all these years has people speculating about what his new sign will say.

I walk a few blocks out of my way to see this new place. He always says he does not see anything funny about his sign. He has an ironic sense of humor. There he is, just as every day, sweeping the sidewalk, humming "O Soli Mio."

As I get closer, I indeed see a new sign in the window:

"The Problem With Italian Food is That
3 Days Later You Are Hungry Again"

"Hey…why you laugh at my sign?"

I just keep laughing.

"You think my sign funny, why?"

"Luigi, I'll be here on opening night."

He shrugs his shoulders and continues sweeping and singing.

I listen to the young boy playing the cornet. *Uno, due, tre.* When I ask them to play something, I exaggerate a bit and feign they have played poorly. I put my hands toward the sky and look up and say, "Mama Mia! I came to America for this?!" The children always giggle, and they seem to like it when I count in Italian, and I, too, like it. It reminds me of years ago, when I first learned to play cornet in that faraway land which is now a vague memory. I have been counting and explaining time signatures for years now, in the same way, for the young students.

I led my life at full crescendo for many years, and have no regrets; I have come to accept that is who I was then. However, the decrescendo that happened due to my automobile accident, marital problems, my experience with Blackfoot, helped me come into my own.

Orsola and I are the last left. Sal, Concetta and Tony died years ago. I walk alone among ghosts of people who influenced me and now are haunts in my mind. They are still with me, for better or for worse.

Orsola is in her 80s now; she is enjoying a nice long life. She still lives in Kansas City, and has cataracts and is blind, and never learned to speak English. She recognizes people by the sound of their footsteps. She still has the great listening skills required to be a musician.

When she writes to me, she tells me about her children, and my namesake, Peter, who plays trombone, and how disappointed she is that he owns a tavern and is not a full time musician. Peter married Frank Basile's daughter, Lena. At the time Orsola was pleased that her son was marrying into a prominent Kansas City family, but it seemed over time Orsola disliked her daughter-in-law because she did not want to move to Denver and Peter never got to perform in my band or any other prominent band. However, she commends Lena for her excellent spaghetti and sense of family duty.

For some reason, all the years I have lived in Denver, no one has ever asked me if I wanted to return to Italy. Not the mayor, President Roosevelt, the mailman, the governor's wife, my students or musicians. There seems to be a sense that Denver is a great place to be. In a sense, I feel like I have returned to Italy. My family and career have been here. I may have been a better-known musician had

I stayed in Europe, but my home is here. So, like my nephew Peter's wife, I understand her sentiment to stay somewhere comfortable.

The last time I saw the Indian girl, whose name was Walk With Me, was around 1923. I heard Mother Cabrini helped her, but in what way I am unsure. The last time I saw Blackfoot was about 1920; I hope he died from natural causes and that he was not murdered at the hand of a European man.

I am told that Mother Cabrini will be canonized as a saint soon; she is quite deserving of this, and of her title, the Patron Saint of Immigrants. She wanted to help people in China, but the Pope told her to come here, because Italian immigrants in the Western United States needed help more than any other people in the whole world. This is so true, and I find it comforting, ironically, that it was not only my own experience, and the experience of my family, that life was difficult here.

Garden of the Titans never really took off the way I had hoped it would. Yes; there are concerts up there and I was the first, but it turned out not to be the internationally, or even nationally, recognized place I had so hoped would put my name even more squarely on the map. But who knows what the future holds?

I have been back there twice for concerts: once when a well-known opera singer came from Europe, and another time when my former student, Henry Sachs, conducted the orchestra there. Henry acknowledged my presence that night, and brought to their attention that my band and I were the first to perform at Red Rocks. Henry has been the bandmaster of the Denver Municipal Band for many years now, and I am proud that I mentored him.

Those rocks will be there for a million more years, and thousands or millions of people could perform there, for centuries: But I, Pietro Antonio Satriano, was officially the first musician to perform at Garden of the Titans, now known as Red Rocks.

Music is so much a part of who I am; I have scores running through my mind. For years, I will get music stuck in my mind and it plays over and over, as if it exists inside of me. When I moved to America and heard ragtime, it got worse. Now I hear the classics, the battle hymns, waltzes, marches and ragtime, sometimes superimposed on each other. It is confusing; what a rich music set I could compose, but the complexity of the composition would be too overwhelming for the ear. Music tends to stick with simplicity, or our minds would not be able to enjoy it. Artists will probably emerge who can mix classics, rag, jazz and opera; Gershwin is very close to succeeding. Satie, and other minimalist composers, are changing the course of music now. In a way, I appreciate it—less is more. But how much less will still equal more? I am happy to have lived through the jazz era. They say it is American music, but when I hear it, I hear the underpinnings of Italian blood.

They waited to hear the music, they waited to see me: Satriano, the bandmaster. The child prodigy. The man who kept getting married and divorced, or the "Young Man with Glasses" as the newspapers referred to me. I loved the newspaper article that stated, "Musical authority indicates Satriano to be the best bandmaster in the country." In thinking about all this, I always felt emboldened and ready to perform.

I liked to arrive early to feel the pulse of the crowd. I arranged my music on the stand, with my back toward the audience. I took my time in arranging the music; my real goal was to feel the pulse of the crowd. My back to the audience got them excited, and sometimes they applauded, perhaps thinking I was going to start the show early or had a major announcement. They loved to see me before a show; it helped build expectation. The more I fiddled with the sheet music, the more the crowd was intrigued. I told my men that I arrived early to make sure they were all sober and ready to play. After Papa was gone, that was really not a problem, and less worrying had been good for my presence on stage.

The city of Denver debated about the way I intermixed both the old airs and ragtime into my performances. Newspapers in the Eastern United States, especially Chicago, kept reporting on our performances. They said I was light on the classics, and my band struggled with simple hymns. I said if the people want rag, we will give them rag. Classical music requires people to think, but most people who came to the park wanted to be entertained, to laugh and forget about life. The Denver City Council gave me five hundred dollars so I could hire more musicians and bring my band up to forty-five men, and I purchased more sheet music to broaden our repertoire.

Years ago, the waltz was considered to be "dangerous" music, even in Italy. Men and women had to stand close together to waltz, and it was believed this dance put immoral thoughts into people's minds, and was associated with women of ill repute. Religious leaders said it was the devil's music, and it reminds me of what my older sister told me about the fortune teller: the fortune teller had the gift of knowledge that came from the devil. After I consulted with the fortuneteller, Orsola worried I would be cursed for life; she believed those things. The fortuneteller in a general way was right about me, but I believe all the hype about ragtime and the waltz were incorrect. The Women's Temperance Clubs of America may frown upon my music and bodily gyrations while performing (and some may object to my occasional body gyrations of a certain nature while not performing), but music is meant to lift us to another level; I did so like the operatic song in German Schubert wrote, "An Die Musik," an ode thanking music for lifting spirits even on the grayest days.

Some people on the Denver City Council have said opera should not be performed on Sundays, because it is too risqué and wicked. There was debate about making a law that it could not be performed on Sundays, but fortunately, there were not enough votes for it to pass. What do these people think the *Bible* is about? They have apparently not read the debauchery that is inherent in the *Bible*, yet many believers tend to for some reason overlook this ubiquitous fact.

Musa died in 1932. A year before, she said we should plan for our funerals and burials. I said I wanted to be cremated. "Oh, Pete!" she exclaimed. "Why on earth for?"

"I want to be different. I will not need my body. I do not believe I have a soul, and if I am wrong, by definition, my soul will be fine without my body."

"Pete!" she said, getting a bit irritated. She slammed down her book, stood up, and put her hands on her hips. "I've had to put up with your infidelity, your long-winded synopsis on the plight and prejudice of Italians, your temper tantrums, all the media attention, and now…wanting your body burned when you die? Why, no one does that."

"Si," is all I said. I can see how Musa would think I am *pazzo*, but I enjoy being different. I told her I would like my ashes to be interned with her.

"Ugh…As you wish." She sat down at the table again.

A few weeks later we went to the Mausoleum at Fairmount Cemetery; it had just opened the year before. It is a huge, quiet white building with beautiful stained glass. The place exudes promise for majestic eternal quietness and solitude. It is said to be the largest building between Kansas City and California. We signed the papers.

The next time I was there was a year later when Musa died. My wife was buried into a marble wall, at the corner of one of the main halls. It was a sad day, but I shall be joining her soon. We grew to be very close and very happy over the years.

I am going through old boxes of things to move to my new home. I will be moving in with Carroll and his wife Bessie. I no longer need a home by myself, and am rather old to live alone. I found some papers of Anna's. Musa always seemed curious about Anna, and it seems strange she never asked me why I had Anna's immigration papers. Anna left them here and never asked for them. Maybe Musa did see them and never said anything. I unfold the old paper carefully and read in large letters:

In the Name of His Majesty Umberto I
By the Grace of God and by the Will
Of the Nation
KING OF ITALY...

It goes on to say that the Minister of Foreign Affairs asks the Civil and Military Authorities of his Majesty and of the friendly and allied powers to freely let pass twelve-year-old Anna...born in Burma and going to Denver (North America)...

Ah, Italy, such pomp and circumstance...

She told me she and her brother read this over and over again when they were on the ship. They thought it was funny and it helped them learn English, reciting this over and over as if a Shakespearean play and using an Italian American dictionary to decipher the words. She would be the Queen, and put a paper tiara on her head, and he would be the King, and put a lampshade on his head. He would stand on a chair and she would bow or kneel before him...

Surely the King had more important things to do than make sure a twelve-year-old girl got to America? Apparently, when I met her in Milan, she was really only eleven or twelve.

CHAPTER TWENTY-FIVE

"There was an ominous pause, followed by a burst of applause.

Satriano was simply Satriano again; the last notes of

'The Holy City' died away in the distance."

Pietro

My life is not as exciting as it once was. I think of myself performing before ten thousand to eleven thousand people and my young body gyrating, jumping, sweating, feeling the pulse of the crowd. Now, it seems my body gyrates, but for all the wrong reasons. I cannot imagine thousands and thousands of people coming to see me from miles and miles away; my body is old now, and is preparing itself for death. I may go see Orsola one last time, and my nephew, Peter.

I listen to the radio a lot, and sometimes one of my songs is played, "Hear the Sammies Coming." It is a march I wrote in 1918, at the end of World War I. After years of my family and I having our musical creations stolen and attributed to other artists, I tired of it and had "Sammies," a slang term for American soldiers, copyrighted with the Library of Congress.

Attendance at musical events is down. Why should people go to a performance if they can see it in the movies, or listen to musical events all over the world on the radio? I am glad I was a young musician years ago. Now, it would be harder to be The Great Satriano, Leader of the Famous Satriano Band.

My lungs have aged, and making beautiful sounds with my cornet is more difficult. My doctor said smoking a pipe so many years has caused my lungs to be hard, and the only time I smoke now is when I occasionally have a gin. My fingers never healed well, but I enjoy playing on my own or with children. I still give lessons and help the Boy Scouts with performances. The children seem in awe of me. Their parents and grandparents have told them who I used to be—that I was the Grrrrreeaat Saaattrrrriaannooo, and I entertained people all over the world, and that I came to America in my early twenties, and I was famous for my temper and my body gyrations and jumping and surprising the band and the audience. I teach them, just the way Papa and Professor Romano taught me: Listen, listen…keep time. Music is about time, and life is about time and what one does with it. I filled my time with music. I am not sure I have much to show for it, but it is the life I led, the life I created.

Now, I go to the picture shows, and I drive my car to Bonnie Brae and have a gin and smoke a cigar. I dreamed of going back to Italy, but that time has passed. At Bonnie Brae, I sometimes see my students' parents, and they say, "How is Joe doing?" Or "We cannot get him to practice, why, that boy doesn't have a lick of sense." Or there are the nervous type parents, who apprehensively ask… "Professor Satriano, do you think he really has talent? Can he really make it…in the musical world?"

"Tell him to listen to music and practice," I always say. The children these days have so many more activities than I did in Europe. Like Carroll, they like sports. And, the parents in America are not as strict as the parents in Italy. If Papa had not forced me, I would have been at the picture shows, fishing and swimming and playing ball instead of hours and hours with the cornet. It is hard to make parents understand the time it takes to learn. They themselves probably do not give themselves time to learn.

I did not get to spend much time with my grandson, who is named after his father, Carroll, but he likes to be called by his middle name, Richard. His parents divorced, and he lived with his mother, and Carroll and I had little contact with him. I feel bad that the problem with women was somehow passed on to my son. Now that Richard is in high school and has more freedom, he comes around to see me sometimes at Bonnie Brae. I tell him stories about the old days, about all the musicians and entertainers who would visit me when they came through Denver on the train. He tells me he would like to be an actor, and I am delighted; it is in his genes, I tell him. He wants to go to college and study acting and philosophy. Before college, though, Richard is going to be in the Coast Guard to help fight the war.

Ah, he got Papa's Jesuit genes, studious and philosophical, yet also wanting to be in the military.

I have been disappointed that the impassioned desire to be a musician seems to have ended with my generation. For generations before me, our people were musicians. I wonder: has the talent ended, or have Sal and Tony and I just been less vigilant in forcing our sons to be musicians?

Richard says, "Tell me one more time, Grandpa, about the first show you did at Garden of the Titans…"

I did not often tell the story of my personal experience at that first performance at Garden of the Titans, but he is old enough now to hear the truth of my experience.

"Picture it: Garden of the Titans, May 31, 1906. A little Italian man standing on a wooden stage. People gathered around listening to my music, my band, in the most beautiful, natural performance center in the world. I composed an original piece, "Garden of the Titans Opus" just for this occasion, and we performed it at the very end. I was thinking, 'God, did I write this?' I know, a funny thing for an atheist to think.

"Before we started performing, I did what Papa told me to do: call forth the angels, speak to them, and they will perform with you. I told my men we were going to call the angels, and make them appear on stage with us; trust it is so.

"I started feeling it during the first song, when I did my signature solo, "The Holy City." Something was emerging, rising, even then. Then, when it was time for "Tannhauser," I was gone, not there, out of my body. I was no longer at Garden of the Titans near Morrison. The music pulsed, pleaded, scorched, cajoled, thrust, acquiesced, teased…it was building into a crescendo like I never experienced in my life. I was at one with the tuba, the trumpet, the cornet, the drums, the cello. They were in me and outside of me, all at the same time. The music and I frolicked, pranced, danced. I was writhing, grimacing, jumping, swaying…oh, God this is good, I was thinking. It intensified even more. I always said classical music is 'thinking,' but if you had asked me at that time, at that moment, I was doing anything but thinking. Classical music is ecstasy and transcendence, and I experienced all those emotions at once, on that little platform, as I performed. Ecstasy, this is ecstasy, I was thinking. Some sort of sublime connectedness.

My body filled with music, until each conjoined note carried me to my own crescendo."

CHAPTER TWENTY-SIX

"Former Band Leader Dies"

May 1946

Richard (Carroll)

My father found Grandpa dead at the piano bench on May 9, 1946. Grandpa had been healthy until just a few weeks before, except that he had lost a lot of weight. Doctors said he had esophageal cancer. He was feverish and weak the morning he died, but was determined to sit at the piano. My father helped him get out of bed and helped him walk on his spindly legs to the piano bench. My father was worried about him and encouraged him to go back to bed, and he did not quite understand Grandpa's last words, "My last wish is to see whether Richard Strauss truly captured the experience of dying in "Death and Transfiguration."

He started playing the piano and composing something with a pen. My father went to the kitchen to get Grandpa some water.

When he came back, Grandpa was slouched over the piano, his mouth agape and his eyes wide, the ink still drying on a fermata.

Acknowledgments

This is a work of fiction. It was inspired by the lives of the Satriano family; however, the portraits of the characters are fictional, as are many of the events described.

Like many authors before me, the phrase "It takes a village" comes to mind and is so true when it comes to writing a book. I acknowledge the following people for their support, encouragement, and insight: Dr. Phillip Carl Chevallard, Holly Slater, Dr. Tarashea Nesbit and Cara Lopez Lee. All of these people were supportive and took an interest in my project and increased my understanding of writing and music that led to the creation of this book. I also thank Elizabeth Cook, the archivist at Regis University (in the story, the original name was given, College of the Sacred Heart), and Michael Allen, president of the Denver Musicians Association. Other people deserving of honorable mention are Paula Primavera at the Covered Treasures Bookstore in Monument, Colorado, Nick Zelinger, David Zuercher, Rebecca Finkel and Brenda Speer.

I thank Cindy Saunders for helping me to love opera and art songs, and expanding my musical horizons and knowledge. She also introduced me to the beauty of the Italian language.

And, a warm thank you to my friend Dr. Cheryl Straus-Witty for being encouraging and supportive of all my endeavors.

I consulted numerous documents in writing this book, among them newspaper articles from the *Denver Post, The Denver Times, Variety, The San Francisco Call, The Catholic Intermountain Newsletter, The Breckenridge Bulletin*, court documents and *Rocky Mountain News*. I also thank Chamisa Redmond at the Library of Congress and Alisa Zahler at the History of Colorado Center.

The books I consulted were:

A Sesquicentennial Celebration: The City of Denver and the Denver Municipal Band, by Gerald Endsley.

Orpheus in the Wilderness: A History of Music in Denver, 1860–1925 by Henry Miles.

From Pavia to Portland, 1845–1892: The Enrico Martinazzi Story and His Descendants, by Toni Martinazzi.

The Italians in Colorado (1899-1900), by Gandolfo Marcello.

Woven into the story are also antidotes from oral and written family history.

While all of the people and documents mentioned provided inspiration to write this book, the impetus mostly came from the Satrianos' interesting lives. I am grateful to Pietro Satriano's great-grandchildren, Michael and Elizabeth Satriano, and to Carroll Satriano, Pietro's only grandchild, for sharing their memories. Liz Satriano, Pietro's granddaughter-in-law, welcomed me into my extended family with warmth and openness.

My thoughts about important family members who contributed to this book, whether directly or indirectly, would be incomplete without mentioning my aunt, Dory DeAngelo, who is known as the champion of Kansas City history; she emulated a passion for preserving and sharing the past. I thank my cousin, JoAnna Cooper (Cona), for her interest in family history and her wisdom in securing family documents for future generations.

And, a nod to the main subjects of this book, my great-great-grandfather and great-great-uncle, Antonio and Pietro Satriano. My hope is that I have done your lives justice. In writing, I came as close as I could to making you come alive again. Thank you for being interesting, talented, and adventurous characters. I am pleased to share your stories with the public. Antonio, I admire you for being a courageous pioneer and forfeiting an accomplished life in Italy to come to America. Pietro, cheers to your amazing talent and passion. You helped shape the musical history of Denver, and beyond. I did my best to convey what I thought your experiences and personalities were like, imbued with a bit of imagination.

Grazie.

Credits

The photo on the back cover is from the *Denver Times*, September 9, 1901.

The cover photo is a family photo of Pietro, taken in Denver circa 1909. Special thanks to JoAnna Cooper (Cona).

The section entitled "Green Eyed Monster Strikes City Park Band" is from an article entitled: Band Leader is Accused of Discourtesy to Famous Visiting Musicians. *Denver Times*, August 23, 1901, page 10, column 3.

The James Joyce poem "*Bahnhofstrasse*," is from *The Complete Poems of James Joyce*. It was originally published in 1918.

The quotes at the beginning of every chapter are from the *Denver Post*, *Denver Times* or *Rocky Mountain News* between 1899-1920, except the last quote in Chapter 26 is a headline from the *Denver Post* on May 18, 1946. All the quotes and this headline are in the public domain. The quote at the beginning of Chapter Six is from the author's family documents.

Author photo credit: Mark Kirkland

Cover design: Nick Zelinger

Interior design: Jordan Tegtmeier, Chappell Art + Design

Made in the USA
Charleston, SC
22 December 2016